MW01602599

GRANDPA VERN

The Ham And The Christmas Tree

Two Black Eyes

A Walk To School

Almond Cakes

A Really Happy Day

The Test

Last Day At The Beach

An Order Of Chicken

A Trip To The Falls

The Bicycle Ride

On The Lord's Pillow
Copyright © 2010 Luis de Agustin
All rights reserved

First Edition January 2012
Printed in The United States of America

ISBN-13: 978-1-453-68982-0
ISBN-10: 1-453-68982-6

On The Lord's Pillow

TEN STORIES OF A BOY AND
HIS IMMIGRANT PARENTS

Luis de Agustin

The Ham And The Christmas Tree

The boy closed his eyes, faced the black sky, and let the falling snowflakes fizz on his cheeks. This was the day with the perfect green Christmas tree he drew on the liquor store calendar above his desk. This was the eve he counted twenty-four nights during prayers, the night he and his father would walk across town to buy their Christmas tree. And just as last year and the year before, he waited at the curb outside Millers Grocery while his father bought two packs of cigarettes.

Up the street, the screech from an approaching city snowplow hurling snow to the sidewalk, spurred the boy from the curb to the grocery store's window, where he watched his father wait at the counter. Soon, his father stepped out with a lit cigarette, turned the corner, and the boy hurried after him.

"I forgot your chocolate," his father said in their native language. "You want this?" He held up a stick of the bitter gum he chewed to help him smoke less.

The boy smiled and shook his head. He slid his index finger into his father's coat pocket and plod beside him over the snow.

In eight blocks, they were at the tree sellers, normally an empty dirt lot now strung with colored bulbs, and afire with empty gasoline drums burning debris to keep the tree sellers warm.

A tree seller wearing a rough fabric coat like his father's, greeted and led them back to where the thin trees leaned against a slack rope. Reaching in and pulling a tree out, then another, the tree seller stamped each trunk twice on the frozen ground and said, "Here's a nice one."

The boy's father motioned the seller turn each tree to show its bad side. They all had a bad side in this section, but the boy learned to hide it against a corner. Except this time, the boy saw his vision of the perfect tree revealed as the fourth tree was turned and turned again. It had only good sides, needles thick, and the tip reached the hanging lights. The boy looked at his father. A perfect tree theirs?

"This one shouldn't be here," the seller said.

The boy's hands slid back into his pockets, and his shoulders sloped.

"But tomorrow's Christmas. Same price as the bare back ones."

The boy grabbed his father's hand.

"Is cost too much," said his unaware father, and the boy accepted the perfect bell shaped tree he drew on the calendar would not be theirs.

But as if the spirit of The Blessed Virgin Mary had touched the tree seller's back collar with the falling snow, he cut the price, and the boy heard his father say, "I take," as he always said. The blue-green, bell shaped pyramid stepped Christmas tree was theirs.

While the seller tied the tree with twine into a cocoon, the boy pictured it in the middle of their apartment's main room. Just like the Christmas show families on TV, they would sit and admire their tree, maybe sip from steaming mugs of Christmas drinks like the fancy people in their joy filled television living rooms.

Best of all, beneath this tree like no other, on a satin cushion he would place the porcelain figure of Baby Jesus his mother brought from her country. This Christmas, plump overhead branches would serve as manger for Baby Jesus.

"See you next year, and Merry Christmas, gents."

Ahead, the boy's father lifted the tree by the thick end, the boy behind at the tip. "Able?" the boy's father asked in their native language, and they left the little forest.

Crossing the town's main street, they were more than half way home. The lights in the shops seemed brighter than the boy had ever seen. The caroling on the loudspeakers carried longer. The rushing shoppers moved out of their way as never before. People noticed a tree like this.

Abruptly, his father stopped. The boy thought it was to let him rest, but before he could falsely say his arm was not tired, looking through the plate glass into Conti's

3

Butcher Shop, his father said, "Look. A cured ham. Like the ones from our country."

Searching where his father gazed, the boy saw an animal hoof hung from a meat hook behind the busy counter. From the hoof grew a parchment brown, kite-shaped slab.

"The whole side of a boar's hind quarters," his father said passing his hand along his hip. And as his father continued speaking and reached into his money pocket, the boy noticed a schoolmate from Catholic school pass beside them carrying a tree with his own father, but a tree half the length of his and narrow as a trashcan. The boy wondered if at Holy Confession he'd need reveal his feelings on seeing his friend's flattened face as it traveled the length of his own magnificent tree; after all, his boastful tree was for the glory of Infant Jesus.

"For the ham, understand?" The boy's father held out a roll of bills like the boy never saw. For sure his father's wages and Christmas bonus rolled into one. "I don't know what it could cost. Take it."

The boy took the roll but not before his father reached to take back several bills.

When the boy asked for the cured ham, the counterman in a white smock said, "The whole thing?"

The boy nodded.

"You sure?"

The boy turned to the store window, but his father was gone. He nodded again to the counterman. A man on line joked, "That boy must sure love ham!" and he and several women laughed.

"Ham it is," the counterman said, and he lifted the side off the hook, placed it on the counter and wrapped it in wide sheets of brown paper. The boy gave him the roll of bills, and the man kept all but two.

A customer held the door open for the boy grasping a ham against his chest the size of a three-year-old child. He stopped on the sidewalk beside their tree, then spotted his father leave John's Novelty Store, and under a street lamp glimpsed he carried a paper bag. Could it be? thought the boy. Could it be the little crib made of twigs tied with twine he requested the Christmas before for his Baby Jesus? Could it?

"What did you do!" his father yelled grabbing the ham. "Two pounds! I said two pounds! What did you buy? Where's the change?"

The boy opened his hand with the two bills. His father smacked it, the bills tossed. "Take the tree."

The boy lifted his end. His father pulled on his cigarette, flicked the butt, and heaved the ham and tree. "Stupid..."

Why couldn't his father return the ham like other people and just try to explain, thought the boy. His father never returned anything.

At the corner, the boy's father dropped the trunk, and pressing the ham against his side, lit another cigarette. Without warning, he lifted the stump and kept walking, the boy now barely able to keep his end from dragging.

Passing the bank where the boy kept his Christmas Account, in two blocks they would be home. Might he have enough in his account to pay his father for the ham, or maybe when they got home take it and return it fast to the butcher for his father's pay?

His father dropped the tree again and stayed still. They stood in front of a lot with an unfinished wood frame house. The ham slid from his father's arm onto the ground. His father leaned as if to cough, then fell into the snow. The boy dropped his end. Bending over the mound of coarse fabric, he called his father. As he did, a figure pushed him away. It was their neighbor with the big white moustache, his piano teacher's father. "Run home and tell your mother to call an ambulance!"

Running in the plowed street, the boy's oversized rubber snow boots held him back no matter how hard his arms pumped. Seeing his row house ahead, he turned to the sidewalk, but scampered up the snow-covered steps to his piano teacher's house. How, he thought, would his mother call and ask for an ambulance? He pressed the buzzer until his teacher opened the door.

*

"Pssst, do you like ham?"

The boy looked up from his stamp collection spread on the small desk his father built.

"I'll make us some fried eggs to go with it," the boy's uncle winked.

He was his mother's brother, and the boy liked him because he said funny things and was not like his father.

He followed his uncle to the kitchen where still uncarved hung the cured ham like a holy icon on their church wall.

"This is a good knife," his uncle said of the fillet knife the boy received last Christmas to take fishing but never used. His uncle pressed the blade to the ham just as the boy's mother bent behind her son and whispered, "My darling, your father wants to see you."

The boy entered the living room and passed the lighted tree. He nudged the door to his parent's room, slid in and saw his father in bed. His father's eyes followed him until he knelt beside the bed. From under the blanket, his father pulled the paper bag from the store across the street from Conti's, and placed it before him.

The boy uncrumpled the end and slowly revealed a crib made of twigs, twine, and tiny silver nails holding a bed of straw.

His head lowered onto his father's tattoo. Through the partially opened door he saw the twinkling lights on the tree, heard the sizzle of fried eggs, felt his father's soft paw press his hair, and soon Baby Jesus would lie in his crib.

7

Two Black Eyes

After the boy twice fell out of bed, his parents set his mattress on their bedroom floor so to be near his faint calls. Next to the mattress on the hardwood floor, his mother plugged in her son's blue box. It played his yellow plastic records, and brought the sleep-filled boy the only friends his burning body knew.

To dampen that blaze, his mother laid cold wet towels the length of his pink body, and on that white shroud, the boy saw snow swans flap winter breeze across a frozen wilderness lake. However, it was his records with songs of cowpokes ridding the frosted range or tales of chilly air rushing by the night caboose, that briefly blew the fire from his body and fog from his head. It was then his eyelids slid open, and as they did, always saw his mother kneeling by his side.

The first of the long needles at the hospital began after he missed five days school.

"It doesn't go any higher!" his mother had wailed on reading the thermometer.

"Can't be!" his father said pulling the stick from her hand, then telling her to dress their son as he rushed to hail a city taxi first time ever.

Afterward, his father took him many nights to the hospital for the long needle with medicine that his mother said would make him well. It was there, they three alone in a room, that he witnessed his father breathe to his mother, "If this does not cure him...," said slow, teeth showing, hand holding her arm tight, while her back pushed against the wall, and her throat gurgled as if a sourball stuck to it.

*

"Toot Toot" and "The Little Red Caboose" were the songs the boy's fatigued arms placed most on his sky blue record player. When The Peter Pan Orchestra and Chorus imitated train engine clatter or whistle blasts, the boy's mother saw her son's lips form the sounds.

But "Round and Round" and "Get Along Little Doggie" were his favorites. On the record label, little boy cowpokes sat around a cook fire, and on the flipside, a boy buckaroo strummed his guitar while a squirrel, robin and pony listened.

If the boy drifted too long, he'd hear his mother's high heals approach. She'd kneel, turn over the record and replace the needle on the grooves. Sometimes, as "Little Toot" or "In The Land of Lemonade and Lollypops" played, because he was unable to drink, she placed her lips to his and pushed cool water from her mouth for him to swallow. Once, when he could not swallow her feed, holding his chin on her shoulder, she quivered, "My treasure, if you were to leave."

His father had warned her about the stray cat, the one with the kitten she had taken in to please her son.

"That cat doesn't look right," his father told her. "Get rid of it. Out of the basement."

She meant only to keep it a short while for her son to play. The mother cat's scratch on her son's chest was such a small thing. The bite on his arm left nary a mark. And after all, when the boy fell ill, the flu was going around school.

It wasn't until after their anxious first visit to the hospital, that she mentioned the scratch and bite to his father. It was then his father raised his fists and slammed the kitchen wall like banging a door where no one is home.

And it was that same night the boy heard his mother tell her sister, who lived on the first floor of the row house, that his father had cornered the cat and kitten in the entrance well to the basement, and with a steel shovel smashed each into sopping pelts. And that after he dropped the lumps in a hole he dug in their yard's dirt drive, he returned, called her, but she stayed quiet, and set the lock on the bathroom door.

That was before the record labels became scuffed from his weak arms sliding the records across the wood floor to place on the player. He would drift off and play with cowpokes and junior engineers, forest animals and talking trains until roused by his worried mother.

But now, his father's voice woke him, and his father's arms slid under his back and legs. And as his father carried him past his mother seated at the kitchen table cupping her face deep in her hands, his heart squeezed.

His father carried him down the stairs. When they passed the door to his aunt's apartment, the door opened. From the dark appeared a gaping tooth hag with long, dirt backed fingernails, who looked like his aunt but whom he had never seen. His father turned and descended the basement stairs, the steps bending into sounds of rat belies bursting.

They passed the room where he and his mother had sat in the old, soft fill couch playing with the cat and kitten. In the boiler room it smelled of heating oil that dripped from hairline cracks his father said could not be mended. At the end of the boiler room, his father climbed the steps to the storm cellar door and pushed it open. Cold winter air filled the boy's lungs.

His father settled him into the wide slat armchair they called "the mountain chair." Frosty air wrapped him. Deep snow covering the yard reflected the moon. Tossing heaps of snow, his father started shoveling.

On no day of hospital treatment did the clinging fog in the boy's head leave as now. Why had they not sat him outside sooner and put out the flames, he wondered.

His father cleared the drive and piled the snow to form a mound half a story high. Standing atop it, he dug a room into the mound that the boy thought would make a place cool to rest.

The chamber finished, slicing the snow along the top of the wall with his shovel, his father carved a row of parapets. After he smoothed the battlement and sloping walls, a castle fort majestically shone.

Lastly, from the base of the snow castle, the boy spotted his father screw out like a beaver through a flurry of snow, clear it, then place a trashcan lid over the castle's secret tunnel. The boy's eyes closed. He sighted a band of captured wild ponies flee through a flung open gate, galloping return to the far sierra. He sighed, opened his eyes, and his father was gone.

Walking to the house, his bare feet left no prints. In the basement, he held the rail at the base of the stairs. He heard his mother in the unlit room. Her outline seated on the soft stuffing couch, he went to her.

She dabbed her nose with a tissue crumpled in a ball. "Darling boy, are you here?"

He told her of his father taking him to the snow and of the snow castle.

"But my darling, it hasn't snowed. Soon perhaps, but there's no snow." Her fingers curled around his wrists, and she gasped, "Your fever, your fever's gone!" And as she pulled him to her, the ceiling light flickered on and she turned away so he would not see her face. To her husband standing at the bottom step, she murmured, "The fever is gone. His color is good." And looking away, with her boy in her arms, she sank into the soft couch.

The next day's light, greeting the boy as he woke between dry sheets, turned his bedroom walls bright white. He listened for the missing cars and trucks on the street. Hastily, he slid from bed, peeked through the blinds, and saw an ocean of snow. Springing down the stairs, dashing through the basement and darting through the opened cellar storm door, he stopped on the snow. Before him stood a story-high snow castle with parapet, sleek turrets flying pennants, and lid covering a secret tunnel.

Bending down, he scooped a proof of snow and held it against his cheek. It stung, and he smiled. His regal manor stood. Puffs of air wrapped the pennants. Adventures defending his castle with knightly friends against snowball barrage and broomstick lance, drifted by his mind like the puffed clouds passing in the sky.

A clinking sound from the side of the house stole his attention. His mother was tapping his bedroom window, his father behind. The boy waved. Her teeth flashed brightly. He looked and pointed at his castle, then glanced back to her, too far to see the dark half moons beneath her hazel eyes.

A Walk To School

Through sun dappled leaves, the boy glimpsed his daily torment, two stocky figures waiting beyond the hanging foliage. They spied him approaching in turn and scampered to their prized places of pleasure.

"There go those two sillies again," the boy's mother said in her native language, walking beside him on the city sidewalk. "They certainly do enjoy themselves every time we pass. Don't you think they're amusing?"

The boy's nervous hand yanked tiny green leaves from hedges along the row houses' miniature front yards lining the sidewalk. When the hedgerows ended, his hand tapped the low brick walls or pulled the wire fences.

"What is it they call to us?" his mother asked. "When you asked its meaning at school, no one knew?"

The boy shook his head and lied.

"Whatever it is, they certainly find it funny."

The boy new the word the twin brothers called his mother. He did not know when he learned it but knew its meaning and that it was bad.

"Darling boy," she fretted, stopping to take his hand. "Look at this cuff."

The hedge leaves had rimmed the edge of his white shirt's cuff green. Spotless, she laid out his school uniform each morning. Unlike other children at Catholic school, he wore his shirts only once, after which she washed, bleached, and ironed them. Good mothers, she said, never sent their child to school with soiled cuffs. "How will you go to school this way?"

Close to his tormentors now, the boy heard them snicker as his mother fussed with and folded his shirt cuff, hiding the dirty, ungentlemanly mark. "Don't let that show, all right, my darling? And tell me what your teacher says about your new tie clip," she said straightening it. "It was your grandfather's. The apple is hand painted red and green enamel, the rest gold."

She adjusted his tie knot, slid her thumbs and forefingers along his navy blue jacket lapels, then stood back admiring her son. "But you haven't said anything about Mommy's new dress," she said pointing to the apple pattern on her low cut summery dress. "We match," she said, and spreading out the hem, half pirouetted to the left and right. "And Mommy's white patent leather shoes, with a high heal no other lady can walk in as well, do you like them?"

Snickering coming from the stoop, the boy forced a smile.

"Thank you, dear heart. Mommy is so proud to walk with the handsomest young gentleman in the city." She bent to kiss him without leavening lipstick, and they continued toward the gauntlet.

There, twin brothers in the same grade as he but from public school, straddled the brick and bluestone sidewalls of the steps leading to their row house. Since spring when weather was pleasant and the boy's mother walked him to school, the two gathered to call his mother the word her ear had mistook to mean a compliment she admired.

When the boys had first daringly called to her, they prepared to flee into the foyer of their house, but she did not react. Days that followed, she did, but instead of being offended, she smiled the smile that normally melted all her son's concerns. She acclaimed, "Yes, I is __," saying the word, followed by, "and happy I is __," repeating the word, thus causing the brothers raucous laughter. And at the end of the boy's ordeal, after he and his more passed just as now, the twins shouted a final, "Hey kid, is your mother stupid!"

"What do they shout?" the boy's mother asked, continuing their walk. "I think being from public school, they're just a little mischievous. Don't you?"

He nodded and pulled the hedge leaves in fistfuls.

*

The boy knew not all public school boys were bad. He knew because after school he played with one. He had met Randy and his father at the model train store.

Randy attended public school but now stayed home, where his father taught him.

He liked trains as much as Randy, but unlike his electric set that traveled only a figure eight track laid on his bedroom floor, Randy's father built him a train country. There were houses, trees and shrubs, water tower and church steeple, tiny people, lots of blinking train signals, three locomotives pulling different line wagons, coal cars, sleepers, and the whole landscape set on a waist high platform covering most of a room. And when he and Randy operated the trains, they got to wear gray flannel caps with silver badges that read, "Engineer."

This after school day, Randy did not answer the doorbell. Randy's father opened the door, and smiling, handed the boy his gray striped cap. "Randy must remain seated today," he said.

Randy waited at the switches for his best friend.

After the boys completed their afternoon's engineering duties, and returned from the distant corners of the country where they took their mighty transports, Randy's father brought them a tray with glasses of cold milk and plates of white powdered donuts. It was the perfect food to fill hungry lineman stomachs, soothe operator muscles, and the only time the boy got to eat food his mother called "not food," but that for him crowned a joyous afternoon.

"May I ask where you got that tie clip?" Randy's father asked. His son had admired it the whole while.

The boy told him his mother brought it back from her country when they went to visit her dying father.

"I see."

It's beautiful," Randy said. "May I hold it?"

The boy pressed the clip releasing the back teeth, and handed the tie clip to his friend. Randy gently rubbed the glow-like enamel apple and its two green sprigs, turned it over and pressed the clip open several times.

"You can have it," the boy said. "It's gold."

"I can! You would give it to me?"

The boy nodded.

"But not going to school or anywhere, I don't wear a tie," Randy said. Thanks, but I wouldn't wear it," and he extended the clip back to his friend.

"It's all right, I have two," the boy lied.

His friend looked up at his father.

His father smiled to each. "Then we need to give you something," he said reaching to a shelf where he kept a prized train engine the boy often admired. Balancing it on its mahogany platform, he handed the finely detailed locomotive to the boy.

Running home from Randy's, clutching his boxed gift, the boy overlooked his mother's eventual reaction at giving away his dead grandfather's heirloom, until he abruptly entered the foyer to their two family home, where unexpectedly, his parents, his mother's sister and husband stood talking at the bottom of the stairs.

Clearly, he thought, they heard he gave away the gift from his dead grandfather from far away, of solid gold, hand made, entrusted to him forever.

His aunt's husband, who knew their adopted country's language, was speaking. "I'm sorry; but that's what it means," he said. "That's what those two are calling you."

"How disgraceful," said the boy's aunt.

His father's already dark expression turned away and started up the stairs to their apartment.

"That's what it means..." his mother said staring far away. "And you didn't know?" she said to the boy as she turned and followed her husband.

*

Long gone was the boy's joy the next morning as his mother led him to school. She did not pepper him with the usual questions about his classmates and teacher, their new country's customs, nor praise him or share the many dreams she held for him. All he heard was the fast tap of her high heels like a hammer striking steel nails into the sidewalk. Ahead, the customary forms scurried to their posts.

"Look straight ahead," she commanded.

The gloating brothers followed their prey's approach. It arrived and they loosened their barrage. Her grip tightened on her son's hand. She did not slow nor turn and smile to the boys, and in an instant the boys were left behind, the brush off provoking loud, newly minted taunts.

"Don't look back," she insisted.

But distressed by the mid-sentence end of the twins' discharge, and realizing they could be coming after them, the boy's head swiveled, and from one eye glimpsed his father's huge figure barrel up the fore steps to the boys' stoop.

"Don't look!"

Neither spoke the rest of the way, except as his mother kissed him goodbye, she said, "Your father will not be home tonight. He has to work extra." And she left unsmiling in the same way and having said the same thing as the last time his father "defended her honor," as her sister later called it. And as he proceeded to class, he recalled the incident that prompted his aunt occasionally refer to his father as "The Enforcer," if only in jest.

It was the year he started kindergarten. His mother worked in a factory where she sewed make believe hair onto rubber doll heads. On days his aunt could not watch him, his mother took him with her to the factory, and he helped her around her sewing machine.

One day as he sat under the machine picking up pins fallen to the floor, a man who worked at the factory leaned over to his mother, and in her language and in a scary way said, "Like I said yesterday, dog bitch, I'll be waiting to fix you."

He remembered it because the man leaned over close to his mother and said the same thing the same scary way three different times. Each time, his mother kept sewing.

Then, just as it was time to leave, his mother smacked the off switch on her machine, and pulling his arm, rushed down not the usual stairs, but a stairway lit with red light bulbs. And when she pushed open the heavy door to the street, standing in the glare almost blotting out the sun, his father's square frame startled him.

His parents stared down the street at the regular exit from the factory. When the man who leaned over to his mother appeared, her chin pointed to him, his father left in that direction, and then his mother took his hand to lead him across a trafficked street.

What he remembered seeing from across the street, was his father approach the man and press him against the side of the building. Then, if he did not imagine it, he watched his father push the man up with one hand, just as Superman did on TV, the man's feet wiggle off the ground, and his father hold him that way while saying something. He then lowered the man, walked him to the fire exit, opened the door and went in with him, the door shutting behind.

Returning home on the train with his mother, she said, "Your father will not be home tonight. He has to work extra."

He did not see his father for two nights, and the next time he visited the factory, he did not see the man.

*

The morning following his father's visit to his wife's young defamers, the boy found his school uniform laid out in the usual manner on the chair in his room, ironed handkerchief on the seat, two wrapped chocolates placed on it. His mother having to work early, his aunt per his mother's instructions made his fried eggs, bacon, warmed cheese, and frothy hot milk breakfast, which moments later sat uncomfortably high in his stomach as he walked to school alone.

Approaching the twin tormentors' stoop, there was no sign of them, and he pulled the tiny hedge leaves ever quicker. Maybe they waited in ambush, he thought. He thought to cross the street, but his mother would disapprove.

He stopped in front of the stoop. They were gone. He looked around. Where could they be, he thought. If they came out of hiding from behind the thick maple or attacked from behind the tin garbage cans, would he keep from running, he wondered.

He resumed walking and once pass the crucible, remembered the chocolates in his pocket. Hopefully, he thought, his father only scared the twins. Wasn't that a face he spotted hiding behind the lace curtains to their front door? Yes, he had seen something move. The boys were unharmed. His father only yelled at them or their parents. They would behave now and never again bother his mother and him. That's all his father did, he thought, as he savored the warmth of the second chocolate.

"Children," his teacher, Sister Mary Joseph said later standing before the seated boys and girls of his class. "I have terrible news. A boy your age from public school died yesterday."

The children turned to one another. The twins' faces crashed like cymbals against the sides of the boy's head. "Which one was it?" he grieved.

"But don't be afraid," she continued, "his soul rejoices in glory with our Lord and Savior, Jesus. His mortal remains however, lie in rest at the funeral home across the street, and Father Gregory arranged for all of you in the boy's grade to pass and view the body in order that you witness that which serves us in this life only, and is of no use to us in everlasting life with our Lord. Let us pray."

The boy bowed his head but did not pray. He thought of his father away and hoped he'd remain away a long time. He had never told anyone that on days his father was away, it was a better day.

When he returned home that afternoon, instead of going to his aunt's apartment, he entered the dark basement and curled on the old soft sofa. When his aunt, looking for him called his name, he hid in the closet until she passed. Later when his aunt and mother found him asleep on the sofa, sleepily he told them he had not felt well. Suggesting all kinds of possible maladies, including not eating enough stewed vegetables, the women changed his clothes, served him a glass of hot frothy milk with crushed aspirin, and tucked him into bed.

*

It was the coffin's glossy brown wood, all the schoolchildren's eyes inspected while they sat in rows in a quiet parlor of the funeral home. The boy admired the long, shiny brass rail that went along the coffin's side. He counted its six balled knobs forward and back. He counted the children in the rows in front of him. He counted the boys alone, then the girls, then repeated.

Sister Mary Joseph clapped her hand, and the parochial school children stood. With each succeeding clap, a row exited their pew and prepared to pass the coffin to view what was in the puffed blue silk.

As the boy's line neared, he watched each classmate slow, turn, and face the box. He could, he thought, look but keep his eyes shut. He was sure that was what his classmates did.

The girl ahead of him approached the coffin, lowered her head, crossed herself and walked on. He slowed, turned, and lowered his head. Gasping like a chugging locomotive, his eyelids began to open. Through a vale of eyelashes, he observed two cupped hands. His eyes traveled over their pale skin, up clean white shirt cuffs and along the blue suit sleeves. At the body's breast, an enameled red and green apple tie clip held the tie. The boy's eyes leapt to the rosy, waxen face. His moist eyes held it until the girl next to him poked him move.

He passed the front row where adults sat, and saw Randy's father. Looking at his son's best friend, the man's lips stretched, and then his arm reached to place something in the boy's hand.

Walking back to his pew, the boy opened his fist and saw a gold key ring with a chain. At the end of the chain hung a train engine sporting red, yellow, and white enamel lights. He slid his sleeve across his eyes, and as he brought it away, saw on the opposite side of the isle where the public school children sat, the twins sitting together. They looked hesitatingly at him, then at the floor.

That night, trying to fall asleep in his moonlit room, the boy heard his father return from wherever he had been. When he appeared, stopping and filling the doorframe to the room, the boy rolled over pretending to sleep. He felt his father come close, and when his lips pressed his hair, the boy squeezed the train charm in his hand until the edges stung.

Opening his eyes, he saw his father move to the moonlit window, look out, hold open his great hands, then bring them spread to his face and bury it in them.

Almond Cakes

High ahead through an opening in the oak and maple foliage expanding like a blossoming portal, the boy glimpsed a blazing image standing on a cloud, Light Onto The World that blessed him each Easter on return from morning mass.

The pipe organ's jubilee still in his ears, he drifted as if floating on a river bound by banks of brick row houses lined with parked cars and neat front gardens. From the white rosebud in his lapel wafted The Lord's Aroma, ascended to glory, His hallowed feet upon a pillow sized cloud.

The glory of The Savior's victory over the cross, remained with him when next he knew he tumbled to the ground. Jubilant in The Lord's feast, he had stopped watching the uneven sidewalk slabs, and his stiff new shoes caught a crack that punished his palms and knees. Durable skin not his concern, he carefully inspected his newly bought suit for frays.

The wool intact, he brushed the sidewalk from his suit, blew on his palms, then spotted the dark crooked crack that caused his fall. Securing his lapel pin, he stood and ahead sighted his father crossing the sidewalk in front of their row house. Instead of his mother on his father's arm heading for high noon mass, two men wearing sunglasses flanked him. At the landing to their home's front door, his mother called his father.

As the men and his father turned to the street, his father spotted his son, and rolled his shoulders to remove the men's hands. As the boy reached him, his mother called to her son in their native language to "Stop them! Hold them! Don't let them go!" and ran into the house.

The two men, tall and thin, wearing black suits and skinny black ties, curled a hand each over his father's arms, then faced the boy. When the boy noticed the handcuffs, his father responded in his native language, "It's all right. They're nothing to worry about. Everything is fine."

Never having seen his father's shoulders any way but broad and flat as a beam, he knew everything could not be fine.

"These men just want to ask me some questions," his father said of the stiff men, and then pressing his bound hands against his waist as if wanting to push them inside his body, turned to one of the men and managed, "Open coat, please."

Instead, the man pushed the detainee to move, but the thick, tree like stock stayed planted. "Tell them to unbutton my jacket," he said to his son.

The boy said it, and one man unbuttoned his prisoner's double-breasted, navy blue pinstriped jacket. The detainee hid his handcuffed hands beneath the jacket's flaps. The men pivoted their charge and led him to the curb.

The boy asked, "Da, will you be back for Easter dinner?"

Again, the men stalled when their prisoner halted. "Of course I will. Tell your mother not to worry. Now go and play – after you give your father a kiss."

However, as the boy neared, an escort shook his head. The boy's father straightened and said, "Your father loves you and will kiss you on return. For now, kiss your rosebud and give that to me."

The boy unpinned the bud, kissed it and handed the flower to a guard. He reached it to the shackled man, whose fingers caterpillared it into his palm.

Then the detainee, or they, turned, and crossed to a long black car where a third stern faced man sat at the wheel. Pushing their prisoner's head down, he settled into the back seat between his companions.

As the vehicle pulled away, the boy's mother swung open the two-story house's front door, saw the car with her husband leave and shouted, "Stop! Stop!" and scampered down the bluestone steps in her brand new high heals. But the car ignored her commands. "Why didn't you stop them!" she called to her son. "I told you to…," she sniffled on a lace handkerchief. "Couldn't you slow them from taking your father?"

As she turned from the street, pushing the lace against her cheeks, the boy noticed a black sock hanging from her hand. It had a knot, and something heavy inside stretched it, as if the bolo was for her to swing at the men.

"On Easter, my God, Easter," she said walking up the stoop.

Watching from the second floor window of the connecting row house, the boy spotted Mrs. Klay, the old woman who never left her apartment, and for whom he ran daily errands.

Rushing out from their foyer, his aunt appeared, dressed for church like his mother in new paschal clothes.

"What's happened, sister?"

"They took him."

"Who?"

"Your brother-in-law, who else. The police. Didn't you hear?"

"I was in back feeding the baby."

"What an Easter. On our way to mass."

"But why?"

"I don't know. From the war I suppose."

The boy's aunt held her sister's head to her shoulder. "He'll be back soon. You'll see."

"He said he'd be back for Easter dinner," the boy said.

"See," his aunt said.

"Easter dinner. Some Easter. How could they. Easter Sunday."

"Come inside. Don't cry; you'll shed your mascara."

"Looks so ugly, mascara when it runs."

Her hand reached to her son, and he slid his in hers and the three walked into the shade.

*

In their upstairs apartment kitchen, the boy and his mother sat at the gold silk cloth covered table she had set for when her husband and she returned from high noon mass having gloried in The Ascension.

She gazed at the plates, silver, and crystal, carafes of sweet wines, and the tray with her husband's favorite treat. The boy watched the snake like black sock with the pipe, resting on the table, about which he thought he'd ask his mother later.

"Many good things in this country, but like our country's almond cakes they have nothing," she said looking at the pastries. "These are such poor imitations."

With her thumb and forefinger nails, she lifted a shaved almond off a pastry and placed the white chip between her front teeth, bit and lightly chewed.

"Let's not wait any longer, my prince. Eat a few now. They're nothing like ours, but sweet just the same, and they please your father."

"Mommy, who were those men?" he asked, biting the pasty almond pastry.

"Here," she said handing him a business card. "What does it say?"

When the boy read the organization the men came from, his eyes widened. "They're from the government. That government agency. The one on TV."

"Which?"

"You know, the one Da and I watch Sundays. Where they shoot and never miss, and always get the bad man."

"Bad man? What are you saying? Haven't I endured enough today? Go change to your regular clothes, and leave your suit for me to hang."

"But Easter dinner at the cousins. Aren't we going?"

"How can you ask. Of course not. How can we go anywhere; not be here should your father return."

"But the cousins," his sticky tongue wined.

"And your father? Return to an empty house?"

She wiped her fingertips on a cotton napkin. "What I don't understand is how they found out about your father, if that's what it is. We've been so circumspect. Cautious. What Judas betrayed him? I'm certain your father in the war is what this is about; actions in wartime these investigators who see life only in black and white, would not understand, nor fathom heroism. On Easter... His hands bound..." She pushed the napkin to her tear duct. "Do you know anything about all this?"

The boy's tongue stuck to the roof of his mouth. He stopped chewing; returned his second cake to his plate. "About...what?"

"How they came to suspect your father? Oh of course not. Let's change, and I'll make you lunch. What kind of mother I am you must think, forgetting lunch. I'll prepare it, and you can have more cakes later."

"I'm not hungry."

"Maybe Da will return by then. Come. Be happy. Give me a kiss my darling boy. My prince."

A lump in his throat, he hugged his mother, the government agents' business card in his hand.

*

Nearing sunset, as his mother saved the celebration's uneaten treats, the boy gazed at the business card and phone number his mother wanted him to call if his father had not returned by nightfall. He thought about the agents, straight and serious, and wondered if they were true like the ones on TV. Those never missed their target, always out-thought the bad men, never hit them, and could always resist the batting eyelashes of women gone bad.

"Your father's back," his mother said calmly.

The boy lurched from the kitchen table but did not see him. His mother stood staring at the entrance door. From the other side came slow creaking of heavy feet on steps. The door opened. The boy cried. His mother left the kitchen for her bedroom.

"Da. Da.," the boy's head pressed against his father's stomach.

"I told you I'd be home for Easter dinner," he said holding his son to his abdomen.

"We didn't go to the cousins."

"Doesn't matter. Wherever you embrace your own, you celebrate the feast."

"Dada."

His mother returned. "What do you want for dinner?"

"Whatever you make."

She pulled a pan from the stove. "Eggs, ham, bacon, chick peas, corn, sausage and pork omelet. Re-heated."

"Sounds like a blessing."

"Only one you'll get from me."

"Then bring me some wine."

"I'll get it," the boy said reaching for the decanter of festive white.

"No. My wine."

The boy reached for the gallon jug under the table his father poured from every night after work, lifted it to him, and the man filled a glass.

"Was it really the government police who took you?" the boy asked.

"Just like on TV."

"Oh yes," the boy's mother said, "and they wore makeup and gave you their autographs." She slid a giant omelet onto her husband's plate.

"Why are you acting like this, woman?"

"Why? Because *I* know what *I* haven't said. Because you must have said something. Boasted, at a card game, or after too much drink or –"

His eyes rose like balls shot from cannon. "I...? Boast...?"

"Then who? Who knows about you here? Who, if he told, wouldn't compromise himself?"

The man reached to his back pocket, drew his wallet, and from it slid an edge worn saint's card. "I don't know."

"But it *was* about the war."

"Yes."

"But you didn't do anything, a crime."

"I know."

"Then what did they want!"

"Co-op-er-a-tion."

Not taking his eyes off the miniature religious painting, he leaned it on the table against his son's rosebud that he slid from his jacket pocket. The boy had seen the holy prayer his father carried, before.

"Saint Barbara, blessed," the man said to the painting of a golden haloed woman erect before a castle tower. His three middle fingers touched the saint's head. "Blessed are you. Again you heard my summons." He swallowed the wine, and then with a bend of his arm, tossed the glass across the kitchen, where it crashed in the porcelain sink.

The interval that his parents stared at one another, was, thought the boy, like the time he was sent to Mother Superior's and sat outside her office waiting for her reprimand.

His father took the postal of his patron saint, who he claimed saved him many times in battle, kissed her head, beamed again with cannon eye at his wife, and gently slid the prayer back into his billfold.

"Did they beat you?" his wife asked.

"They don't do that here."

"They don't know what you went through; what three wars are like."

"Drop it."

"They think in black and white, just like their rancid suits. Imagine – Easter Sunday."

"Son, bring me the leather portfolio with my commendations."

The boy scrambled and left the kitchen. Befuddled, his mother turned to her husband. He lifted the gallon jug and poured.

When the boy returned holding a stiff leather folder and saw his scrutinizing parents, he realized he belied knowing nothing of how the authorities heard of his father's past in another country.

Putting the jug down, his father's hand reached to his stunned son. "It's all right. Come. Bring it here."

The boy approached and handed his father the flat folder.

"This was not for you to see, or show," his father said.

"I only showed it to the kids from the street."

"Who gave you permission... to rummage... ruin... wreck...," said his mother.

"But. They're just drawings of Da's medals."

"That I should have destroyed," said his father, "but vanity..."

"Vanity?" she said.

"It's my fault," he said.

"Vanity," she said. "Where was vanity when you gambled the trophies that went with that folder on a hand of cards? Vanity, the one who won battle medals sitting at a card table. Not vainglory in that folder, husband, but memory. Testimony to steadfastness. Acts of courage remembered."

"Reviled, here."

"Deeds of courage."

"Whatever you say. Just, drop it. Forget it."

"Must we forget everything here? Own no past. Purge every noble deed from memory. Are we, am I, to keep no past in this scrubbed and purified land where only the future matters? Your son know nothing? We, hide everything? Until completely forgotten, even to us?"

He nodded. "Even to us. That's the price." He stood.

"What are you doing?"

"Move aside."

Lighting a cigarette, he walked to the sink, portfolio in hand, flipped the cover and took a yellowed sheet.

"No you're not," she snarled and bound at him.

His cigarette pressed the paper.

"No!" she pleaded reaching for the flaming paper.

"Off," he pushed her.

"Why destroy them?"

He held her off, grabbing more sheets he lit page on page.

She held her tears, until the last commendation, one that unfolded several times. "Even that one, reckless man? What loathing you can bear destroy even that one, from the commander himself. Are you above the crown?"

"There are no crowns here."

"Sure, everyone is equal here. Until they take you in handcuffs. Then you have the rights of a grub off a freighter. A grub. A nothing. A grub with no past. A nothing grub."

The long document aflame, she lifted her head, "You couldn't even save that one. For my sake."

"Let it go and move on. This malignance won't hurt us anymore."

"Glory; which you maligned."

"That shadows my door no more."

"What a wretched country of simple men, simple hearts and simple heads. So plain, everything here. Everything easily separable. Nothing complicated. All divisible by two. Why did we come here? Why, husband, did we settle in this pure and simple land of no past?"

The flame out, the boy's father dropped the char of the last document into the sink. The folder emptied of its decorated past, his father turned the faucet on and the ash washed down the drain. Above the sound, the boy heard his mother's sobs. When she turned, her comely face, normally smooth like the exalting saints, looked like the martyred. Gasping from the base of her ribs, she headed for her bedroom, passing her son, "Why did you do this?"

The faucet's fizz ended. The boy's father dropped his cigarette in the drain, then dried his hands. "I'm going to your mother," he said. "But first, do you remember that little fort you built out of wood, with the insignia along the front that I told you were a bad thing, and to never draw again? Did you destroy it as I said?"

The boy nodded.

"Good. That insignia is a bad thing you should never draw, praise, or have in the house. Everything will be all right now. I'll go to your mother. She'll calm down, and later you and I can watch that show you like with the government policemen. They never miss their target, eay?" and he ruffled his son's hair.

Soon as his father closed the door to their bedroom where his mother still cried, the boy shot down the stairs to rectify the lie, destroy the fort he'd built with the funny insignias he'd drawn on the gates and watchtower.

*

When he exited the house, it was near twilight, and for the first time ever, he saw Mrs. Klay away from her upstairs apartment. Her grown son, and husband, Dad Klay, carried her down the stoop in her wheelchair. The boy slowed at the sidewalk and waited for them to set her down.

"Has your father returned?" she asked.

"Yes, Mrs. Klay."

"Three days ago you showed something to your friends you shouldn't have. We should all be proud of our parents. Your father, a soldier, did his duty, but not everyone sees things the same way. Objects kept hidden, are so for good reason. I keep a relic of St. Patrick. It keeps snakes from wrapping around my decrepit bones. Not even Dad here or my children know where I keep it. If they found it, they might say I'm a crazy old coot keeping a cut off fingernail, and have me carted away. But my belief in my holy relic is what holds me true to this life, untrue and deceptive as it is. Your father, I've seen, and he's upright. Handsome man too. Big hands remind me of Dad as a youth – though Dad never had a moustache. Anyway, Dad here, because he's a retired cop, the parents of a boy you showed your father's papers to with drawings of glorious medals, came to inform us we lived next door to war criminals – your mother, it would seem by association – and they wanted to know what to do about it. Dad of course told 'em off. What did you tell 'em, Dad?"

"I told 'em to get out of my house."

"Dad knows character."

"Told 'em I'm an excellent judge of character. Forty-one years on the force, you see every kind, and that your father was no bum, and they should mind their own business."

"They, it turned out, had a different idea of people's business," she said.

"Went to the feds. Everybody who knows nothin', that's where they go."

"Feds," she said.

"The fancy boys."

"With the skinny ties."

"They got their butts in theories, and eyeballs in microscopes. Poor intersection to figure character. But because nothin' can stop big wheels turnin' once they start, your Dad got his visit."

"Give me your hand, child."

The boy did.

"Your dad is innocent of whatever they say. You believe that don't you?"

He nodded.

"But your father can't try and fight 'em," Dad said. "or they'll put the clamps on 'em for sure. Jail 'em, then send 'em back to China."

"He ain't Chinese," Mrs. Klay said.

"I know he ain't. And you know why you can't fight 'em. 'Cause they fight to win, any way they can. Bein' defeated ain't part of their nature. Right, Mom?"

"I don't know, but discretion can certainly be the better part of valor. Be good," she said to the boy. "Let's go Dad. Jerr. Happy Easter, child. What's left of it."

"Bye, Mrs. Klay. Bye Dad."

"Bye."

The boy watched them lift Mrs. Klay off the chair and onto the front seat of her son's car, and after they got in, all waved, and he continued to where he set out.

At the alleyway to the garages, he turned. He walked on the spare gray gravel to the last garage, behind his house. It wasn't a garage, but a carport his father was building for the car he planned to buy. The boy stopped at a sand pile.

His father hadn't originally told him to destroy the fort he'd built, just "remove those symbols" because they were "bad" and he should "never draw them again." He had copied them from one of his father's commendations, but he'd previously seen it on TV and war movies. After his father's objection, using a razor blade, he cut the swirling symbols off the fort.

He liked the dancing spiral, bold and simpler to draw than any of the other commendations: the red cross with laurel; starburst decoration; the white and blue circle with arm and ax; five point gold star; purple and green flower; knight in armor; St. James with the single word "Valor" on the back in his parent's language.

His hands reaching into the sand, searched for the fort. Pulling it out, sand streamed from it. A breeze whisked the finer powder, and it reminded him of the movie "Beau Geste" when desert sands bury the fort and it's later rediscovered, like a treasure found, which was why he buried his fort in the sand.

But unlike the movie's fort reawaked beneath the desert sun, his foot loomed over his fort before crushing the hand cut plywood. Back and forth he worked his soles. When he finally looked down, he saw only splinters and bits of corner joints where he had added extra glue.

Like a thresher gathering field's wheat, his fists bundled the debris, reached through an opening in the unfinished wall of the carport, and tossed it into the back lot of the food market behind their yard. There, among discarded bottles and wrinkled corrugated board, his painstakingly built desert fort disappeared forever.

When he returned home, his mother and father sat at the kitchen table, she with the cup of the leafy tea she drank "to calm my nerves that stupid people put on edge."

"Did you do that?" his father asked him.

He nodded.

"Sit."

He sat on one leg, the other dangling almost to the floor.

"I feel better now," his mother said to her son. "Forgive me for before. I was upset."

The boy nodded, and his bent leg slid down and swayed with the other.

"Those men," his father said, "will return. Don't be afraid. I'll speak with them, and that will be all. Clear?"

"Yes."

"What you found and showed your friends were the certificates of medals given your father," he said.

"Won and awarded," his mother interrupted.

"Those aren't things you want to win," he responded.

"They were honorable acclamation," she said. "Nothing to hide or shame," she added to her son.

"But," his father continued, "here, they might not understand, because other men who your father served with did ugly things under the same banner, wearing the same uniform. It's them the gentlemen from this morning want."

"And they want Da to identify one," she said.

"But I didn't serve with that kind."

"Nevertheless, there's a man they think is one, who Da knew. You actually know him."

"The little man who tells jokes and gave me the train set?" the boy smiled.

"Him," she said.

"But he was not one of those men. He was valiant. I served with him. And to the truth of his innocence in war, I'd place my neck," he said using two fingers like a blade cutting the back of his neck.

"But another man told a different story," she said. "And if your father will agree, the government men will leave Da alone and forgive him for not reporting like he was supposed to when he arrived here, that he served in the army he served in. That's what's happened. Do you understand?"

"And will Da tell on his friend?"

No, dear. He won't. If he did he wouldn't be the person whose folder you found," she said turning to her husband.

His head lowered and stared at his folded hands.

The boy contemplated the kitchen floor with the brick imitation tiles his father laid, the decorative separating wall for flowerpots he built, the cupboards he cut, the shiny wallpaper with rows of daisies he hung.

His mother sipped warm leafy water from her cup as her eyes fixed on the wall ahead, on a single daisy, and a single round yellow center dot in the daisy, a speck of an idea seeding in her mind.

*

After school the next day, the boy hurried home, his science paper on "The Planets" in his hand. He received a 99% and a single comment from his teacher penciled next to his drawing, "Mars should be red not purple," and the Martian antennae sticking out of the sphere crossed out.

Seated at her usual second floor window, Mrs. Klay, seeing him up the street, waved him "hurry."

The boy passed the long black car parked in front of the house, the driver asleep.

"They've been in there a while. Your father could use you for sure," she said.

He leapt up the stoop, ran through the foyer doors and up the stairs, heard voices from inside his home as he approached, but then unexpectedly stopped. On the landing, pushed against the wall, his plastic green soldiers lay in a heap. He liked assembling them in platoons on the steps and landing, attacking positions or defending against marauding invaders.

After a battle, he lined them abreast, but someone pushed the formation into a pile. Some in the bunch bore red blotches. These were his dead or wounded. With poster paint, he colored where they got hit. After each battle, he chipped the paint off with his fingernail, and they'd be fresh recruits, in new fatigues, the wounds of war gone.

As he slowly pushed open the apartment door, the voices inside untangled.

"Oh come on! You're getting insulting. Here's a sworn statement to the fact from a vetted witness!"

The two government agents of the day before and his father each sat at a side of the kitchen table. His mother, standing next to his father, on seeing the boy enter, dashed from the room.

His father asked him in their language, "What's the word for rat?"

The boy answered, and his father said, "I no is rat. I no is Judas," to the agents.

"Come on in, son," the first agent turned to the boy.

"You can be a big help. You know who we are, don't you?"

He nodded.

"Ever see us on TV?"

"We like your show."

"And you'd like to be an agent," said the second agent.

"No. A soldier."

"Ahh, like daddy. That's good. But we're really in the same kind of work. Fighting injustice. That's what your dad says he volunteered for, in the big war. And we need cooperation from people to do just that, fight for what's right. And your father can help."

"Look at this," said the second agent holding his wallet badge to the boy. "The real thing."

The boy thought it looked a lot like the drawing of the five point gold star awarded his father.

"Seems like a good boy you got there," the first agent said. "Catholic school, huh?" he said referring to the boy's school uniform.

"Is good boy."

"And all you need do to keep him there, and his mother and you in this country, which took you in, asking nothing in return but that you follow the law, is cooperate in tracking down criminal element. Just agree that the man already identified by one of you guys is who we say he is."

"This man no is criminal."

"You don't realize the hot water you're in. You came into this country, signed a paper and swore you never served in a foreign army that had taken up arms against this country. That was a lie, which you now admit. That will land you behind bars for a long time, after which you get booted back to the mother country."

"And of course you think that pretty wife will wait for you."

"I is no lying. This man hero."

"Sure. You're all heroes. Everybody's innocent. Got chests full of medals for being innocent. Big heroes, then. Guests of this country now, looking at jail time, then deportation. We're not like on TV!"

"And we'll find more stuff on you!"

"You know what I mean, de-por-ta-tion? Bye-bye? Leave all this? Pretty wallpaper, well fed kid. Go back and dig sod, shovel horse manure, whatever to survive back there – considering your side lost."

"No washing machine in the mother country. How long you think your pretty wife's manicured fingernails will last, or if the perky thing's going to stay with a broke felon like you?"

Suddenly, with ra-tat-tat like gunfire, the boy's mother's high heals transported her back to the kitchen.

"What party is she going to?" the boy wondered.

She had changed into a festive flowered print, painted on a swath of glowy lipstick, and her loosened hair filled the room when she tossed it as she did. And taking a little mirrored case from her glittery purse, she dappled on skin colored powder from a pad as the men watched. She then pressed her lips looking at the mirror, snapped the compact, returned it to her purse, and adjusted the folds of her dress along the boa constructor belt.

"I take son piano," she announced. Then quickly to her son, "Get your lesson, I'll be walking."

Moments later, piano lesson in hand, the boy met his mother as she left her sister's downstairs apartment and her sister with daughter in arms closed the door.

"Come on, we're in a hurry," his mother said.

They rushed down the stoop, his mother stepping sideways, and three houses down, arrived at his piano teacher's.

"Go in and pay attention," she said continuing, then turned back forgetting something, and kissed his cheek. "Now go."

She left again but the boy remained watching her moving almost at a sprint, navigating the uneven sidewalks, admiring her sway, one he had noticed others admire as well.

"Where are you going?" he called.

She did not answer.

"Where are you going!"

She waved without turning.

"Mommy!"

She kept going, but the piano playing inside his teacher's living room stopped and his teacher's head poked out the open window. "Did you want to start early, today?"

His attention on his mother, he did not see his teacher, but when he spied his mother turn into the alley to the garages, he rushed up the stoop to the door and repeatedly pressed the buzzer.
When his teacher, a recent music college graduate who lived with her parents, answered the door, he asked, "Can I use the bathroom?"

As he hurried through the kitchen, his teacher's mother called, "I made the powdered sugar cookies you like."

He'd passed but took three steps back and thrust his head into the kitchen, said "Thank you," then continued to the bathroom, but not before passing his teacher's white mustachioed father seated at a roll top desk in his room, who said, "Yiassou," followed by the boy's name as the boy rushed by.

The boy locked the bathroom door, spread the window curtain facing the garage alleyway, and waited.

The bathroom smelled like roses. He noticed a bowl full of red petals, brought the fragrance closer, then saw his mother pass.

In between Mrs. & Dad Klay's and another garage, she stopped and approached a shoulder high concrete wall. She kicked off her high heals and grabbing the top of the wall, pulled herself onto the ledge. When she jumped down the opposite side, he lost site of her, but he knew, he thought, where she headed. After the government agents took his father, she left the sock containing the pipe on the kitchen table. He asked her if she would have hit the agents with the sock. It turned out that "the pipe," she told him, was a roll of gold coins. She and his father had brought it with them to use in an emergency.

Couldn't she have used something else to hit the agents with, he asked, and she laughed and petted his cheek. She told him he must never reveal their golden secret. The sock was buried in a sealed coffee can at the base of the telephone pole along the separation between Mrs. Klay's and another neighbor's garage.

His mother reappeared and leapt from the wall to the gravel.

"Are you all right?" his teacher's mother asked outside the bathroom.

"I'm almost finished."

"I have cookies for when you finish your lesson."

Brushing herself off, his mother slid her heals back on. As she walked past the window, she kept straitening her dress, and in her hand he sighted the black sock.

His hour piano lesson done, he hectically licked the Greek cookies' sugar powder from his fingers, promised he would practice the Mozart an hour every day, with Sunday off, and returned headlong to his house.

On entering the first floor, he saw his aunt rushing down the stairs from his parent's apartment. Wearing equally long high heals as his mother, she grabbed the rail and skipped sideways down the steps, a single deep line popping on and off her slender calves.

"I can't kiss you," she said, and he supposed it was her lipstick. "Come." She took his hand and they stopped outside her apartment door where his cousin lay gurgling in a playpen.

His aunt ran into her apartment and soon reappeared with a baby bottle. "Here, watch." She picked her daughter up and gave her the bottle, which she took, sucking the rubber nipple. "Hold her until she finishes. She'll fall asleep and you can put her back in the pen and cover her with her blanket. All right?"

"All right."

"Good."

She kissed him with her cheek and scurried back up the stairs. As she went, she took a cigarette from inside the

53

top of her dress, and slid it into what resembled a long pen, holding the pen between two outstretched fingers. When she opened the upstairs door, he heard a scream, a cackle, then the door slam.

Before the last of the milk in the bottle was finished, his cousin's eyes closed and the nipple left her mouth. He lowered the baby into the playpen and pulled the blanket to her chin, wondering if the thudding upstairs would wake her.

Standing at the top of the stairs, he waited at the shut door and listened to the commotion behind.

He turned the doorknob, slowly pushed the door, and the noise erupted. Inching into the kitchen, he saw the still seated agents, but with their jackets off, ties loosened.

His aunt stood dancing, if that's what it was, on a chair, and as she shimmied on the balls of her high-healed feet to music, the agents convulsed, clapped, and blew smoke from cigarettes leaning off their lips. Everyone held a glass, and on the table and shelves stood liquor and beer bottles.

When his father, still at the table, saw him, he slowly slid off the soldier's V cap he wore, but as his mother appeared and passed him, she swiped the cap from his hand. She slid it onto her head smiling at the agents, and with one hand on the low, kitchen separator wall, leapt to sit on it, the red and gold tassel at the front of the cap swinging jauntily.

He had never seen his mother smoke. Each time she drew from the cigarette holder even longer than his aunt's, her neck leaned back and tousled her billowy chestnut hair. When she blew the smoke, her crossed legs swung as if kicking on a swing, and somehow the strapless high heals hanging from her toes did not fall off.

This was the party his aunt and mother must have dressed for. They were enjoying themselves, because they all laughed, raised glasses, and the agents whooped things like, "You S.O.B.'s are all right!"

When his aunt leapt from the chair, she grabbed a glass of bubbly wine and jumped onto an agent's lap as they both laughed. On the table, the black sock looked like a snake with a neat row of gold guts spewed out its mouth.

"You know," the first agent said smiling at the boy's father. "We never wanted to take you in."

"Yes," the boy's father said.

"Your name gets on a list and we have to."

"Our job," said the agent holding the boy's aunt.

"You checked the most convenient box on an immigration form. But any opportunity to get corroboration on a suspect, we have to take it."

"Is land of opportunity."

"That's right."

"Is much opportunity here," the boy's aunt said, pushing the second agent's hair back.

"You people are all right," said the first agent. He lifted his glass, and all followed. "To good people, and opportunity."

"An' good drink," smiled the boy's father.

"And bad women," said the other agent, as they laughed and downed their drinks.

Putting his glass down, the first agent moved to stand. "Our report's going to say you know nothing about the accusation on this guy. You came across him like you did a hundred other guys in your division on any given day. That likely it's a case of mistaken I.D. and the guy's nobody."

"Yup," said the second agent sliding on his jacket while the boy's aunt did his tie.

"There's a lot to be said for loyalty and comradeship like yours."

"And defense of your country," added the second.

"And being a good soldier, as clearly you were. Fighting for ideals. I, we, have to respect that," he said pointing back and forth to his fellow agent while his other hand lifted the end of the sock and emptied the balance of the clinking coins onto the table, which he swept into his palm and dropped into his jacket pocket. "Because respect is all it comes down to."

"This true," said the formerly accused.

"We got to go."

"Ohh, so soon?" said the boy's aunt, throwing her arms around the agent with the gold in his pocket. "But you come back?"

"No."

"Oh… this terrible."

"Party's over, so don't wait."

"All right, we no wait," said the aunt, and laughed.

"So long."

"Stay out of trouble."

"We see you in the TV!" the boy's aunt called.

Fastening their jacket buttons and sliding on their sunglasses, the agents walked down the stairs with all their previous decorum.

The boy's mother closed and locked the door, then exhaled long enough, thought the boy, to blow out all the candles in church. "Did we lower ourselves, sister?" she said plopping into a chair.

"There's no shame in saving a man, her sister said. "Is there, brother-in-law?"

"I see two gallant combatants," he said raising his glass in toast. "Battle weary but hardened."

"We hardened long before this," his sister-in-law said.

"I know," he said, bringing his wife to his side. "Almond Cakes," he said pressing her hair and using her pet name.

"Mommy," said her son, who she put her other arm around.

"Still, I feel mortified," she said to her sister.

Her sister's round cheeks slackened. "We played roles for a moment. They were not us. We're no less. You saved a man's, your husband's conscience, and another's scalp, who once saved his neck and other men's as well. You feel dismay? When since landing here like a sack of potatoes don't I feel like a slug making way through jungle?"

"Dignified, this existence always isn't."

"Remember when we were teens, after going to the movies we all wanted to visit Hollywood some day and become actresses? We had the looks. Well today we got our screen tests."

"I think we passed."

"So cheer up. Your family's together and your husband is still the man you married, and you needn't live with having betrayed someone. Don't you agree that would be harder to forgive than playacting one afternoon?"

"You're right. I'm feeling sorry for myself. We acted as others only think they'll act, when called. We didn't betray. Kept our dignity. It wasn't so bad."

"You got to wear your party dress!"

"Heals and lipstick too."

They hugged. "You'll make me ruin my mascara."

"There," the boy's aunt said kissing her sister's hair.

"How dull I sounded."

"Everything's turned out for the best. You even have a batch of real almond cakes."

"Oh! I forgot!" The boy's mother suddenly perked. "Darling boy," she motioned to her son, "behind the bread, bring it here."

And while the boy went where his mother instructed, his aunt opened her hand over the table and dropped seven gold coins. "So it wouldn't be a complete disgrace," she smiled

Her brother-in-law laughed.

"You owe me big for Christmas," she grinned.

"And how."

"I'm sorry I brooded," the boy's mother said. "So ungrateful," she added as the two embraced.

"What do you have there then," they called to the boy carrying back an embroidered silk covered tray.

"Almond cakes," he smiled. "The ones Da savors," and lifting the cloth, he revealed the pastries arranged in concentric circles.

"The real ones," marveled his father. "How? From where?"

"Your friend left them this morning," his wife said. "His sister arrived by plane, and he had requested them for you."

The freed man took a pastry and handed it to his son, then others to his wife and her sister, then himself. "What sweet fortune ours," he said, "arriving in this abundant land. Favored we, carried always on The Lord's pillow." And as those he delighted in bit the savory treat, his moustache spread.

A Really Happy Day

Again the swimming pool's turnstile stuck, prompting a rolling moan from the hopeful pool goers. Except for the crooked line the boy and his parents lingered on, through the bank of rotating turnstiles streamed masses of workweek-freed city dwellers. Like sand through a sieve they escaped their week's impoundment for the water's cool libation.

This was the biggest pool in their adopted country, the boy's aunt had told his mother. On a hot Sunday, twenty, thirty thousand visitors arrived, and if he got into trouble, his aunt warned him, no one would know, so the boy stayed near his parents.

"Don't forget, first thing is apply sun lotion," the boy's mother said while checking her lipstick in a compact mirror. "You won't forget, will you?" she poked her husband.

"No chance with you reminding me at least four more times, I'm sure," he smiled dragging on a cigarette.

"Never tempt what can harm you," she turned to her son. "And do watch your cigarette," she added to her husband, "the man in front of you almost backed into it."

"We're moving," the boy's father said.

"Take your pool bag, dear," she told her son.

He lifted the bag she packed with his "pool garments" that included slippers, brimmed cap, terrycloth robe, change of neatly folded clothes, and "after sun cream."

His father carried his mother's low folding chair plus a blanket, and a towel-packed satchel.

"We're next," she said, approaching the manned turnstile. "You have the tickets?" she asked her husband, and as he turned to answer, the turnstile stuck, the man in front him stopped, and his cigarette pressed into the man's back.

"Damn!" yelled the burned young man. "What you do!"

"Keep moving," the attendant said forcing down the turnstile arm.

The young man, followed by the boy's father, the boy and his mother, passed through the turnstile.

Half surrounded by other tattooed toughs, the burned youth waited in the middle of the concrete concourse to the pool.

"You burned my back, man! You stupid?"

"I sorry," responded the boy's father.

"Sorry? Look at the hole in my shirt, man. That's silk. You know what that costs, you stupid fool?"

"I pay."

"Damn right."

"How much is?"

"More then you got in your sorry ass-wallet."

"No worry. I burn hole. I pay new."

"Show the cash and maybe we don't whip it off your sorry hide."

The boy's father flicked his wallet.

"How much you got?" asked the youth.

"I has..." He turned to his son and in his native language asked the word for fifty.

His son replied, and his father said, "Fifty," to the tough.

"That ain't near enough, but it'll do." His hand reached to the wallet, two fingers pressed the bills together, slid the package out, then shook it like a fan in front of the boy's father. "Stay out of our way today, pops."

"No worry."

The scoffing tough and his gang strutted past the man their size and half again, and swaggered down the concourse.

"Did you just give away all our money?" the boy's mother asked her husband.

"I ruin a man's shirt, I pay for it."

"Noble. But the one day that in order to please our son's wish to not bring our own food, and instead eat what they sell here, you leave us without money."

"Apparently."

"Apparently?"

The boy saw half smiles form.

"Well then," she turned to her son, "Apparently, you won't eat lunch today. "And," she turned to her husband, "your cigarette, dear, is snuffed."

He eyed the bent, extinguished smoke he still held coolly, nodded, then flicked it.

"Come on," she said. "Let's find a nice place for Da to rest his great big head – which I'm glad he kept. Although… it might at least have negotiated."

"Better to take the short odds than tempt fate."

"You?" she grinned arching her eyebrows. "Never mind. I'll figure out something for lunch."

"Wouldn't be you if you didn't," he said.

*

From the gray concourse, they passed onto sky-blue painted pavement. It surrounded the lake-size pool thought the boy, like a city train's waiting platform loaded with commuters.

"My sister wasn't joking," his mother said. "There's not a stint of shade. How can they build a magnificent pool like this and not plant a tree or offer a shady place?"

"Maybe the sun lotion companies had a vote in it," her husband teased.

"You think you're tough, but it won't be funny when you burn like a red pepper. Keep walking. We're sure to find something."

"Mommy, I think I see grass way at the end."

"I think you're right, darling."

They continued advancing through the bathers, and then she paused. "Look at that diving platform. Three, no, four levels!

"The top one, is that a hundred feet high?" the boy asked.

"Definitely."

"Did you ever dive off one that high, Mommy?"

"Sure."

"You weren't afraid?"

"Your mother afraid?" his father quipped.

"There was one that high near my parents' home. As a little girl, I got to know it from my window. Then I started practicing on the low board, and in time made it to the top platform. You should have seen me. But that was before the war. I was a champion then."

"A regular Esther Williams, no?" her husband teased.

"An actual Esther Williams!" she said.

"Who?"

"A bathing beauty like Mommy, who dove from high places in the movies," his father said.

"And Mommy is like her?"

"I don't know. Let's see, Mommy," her husband coaxed.

She neared the edge of the pool, spread her arms, tossed back her hair and posed as if for a calendar. "Esther Williams," she smiled. "Don't you think?"

"You outdo the poor thing," her husband responded.

"You think so?"

"Beside you she'd dive into the water to hide her tears. Maybe never come up."

"Go on, you flatterer."

"And look, Esther, there's your spot of cool meadow," he said pointing his chin where the boy earlier pointed. "It awaits your heavenly splendor."

"Then prepare the way," she said dramatically spreading her hands into another pose to end the show, and the three walked toward the green spot.

*

"There's a fence in front of it," the boy said referring to a tall wire fence blocking their destination.

"Da will pull it up and we'll crawl under," his mother said.

"Is that a river on the other side?" the boy asked.

"It's a sea inlet," said his mother. "You don't want to go in that water though. Your aunt says it's filthy."

The fence at pool's end, separated the municipal complex from a strip of spotty grass before a rocky jetty and wide inlet where barges and tankers plied on tar looking water.

"Can you lift it?" she asked her husband as he bent a portion of the wire.

"I think so but we're sure to be arrested."

"Don't be such a scaredy."

"I'll tell them you made me do it."

"Go ahead. I'll contend with them just as I contend with you."

"I pity those cops then," he grinned.

"You know you won the lottery with me."

"I know," he said, and continued lifting the fence waist height, under which they passed to the grassy side.

"This is lovely," she said. "Look at those boats, dear," she said to her son.

"Did you come on a boat like those?" he asked.

"How absurd," his father teased. "We came on The Queen Marry. Didn't your mother tell you?"

"No we did not, but it was a lovely boat."

"Except the captain had to get out and push once in a while – when he wasn't shooting pelicans for dinner."

"Don't listen to your father. It was a grand boat, with fine food. Now everybody apply their lotion, and we'll go to the pool."

"You both go. I'm going to first sit here and enjoy the scenery from your chair – if I may," the boy's father said.

"As you wish if that's what you want to do this beautiful day," she said.

"Six shifts at the brick factory and four at the flourmill, 'lounge' is what my arms, legs and back say do." And as his wife and son applied their sunscreen, he spread the blanket, lit a cigarette, and settled into the low, folding chair.

When he woke, he was staring down and saw the ash from his cigarette mixed in his chest hair. As he lit another, he watched two fishermen standing on the jetty handling long rods. He stood, hunched under the bent fence and walked to the pool.

Around the diving area, he scanned a crowd watching someone climb the stairs toward the third level of the diving tower. "Who could it be?" he smiled to himself. And as he walked behind the crowd, he heard a woman wearing a straw bonnet with pink flamingos and the words "Florida Is Fun," say to another, "That's Esther Williams, you know."

"Really? Esther Williams? Shouldn't she look a lot older?" the spectator answered.

"Oh you know how these Hollywood stars are pampered and preserved, taking advantage of every youth and beauty treatment. And with the personal trainers and snip-snip doctors they employ, they're kept young practically forever."

"But what's she doing here?"

"Raising money for charity."

"Oh?"

"Yes. Haven't you made a donation?"

"No, I –"

"Well I'm collecting for her. It's whatever you can give. It goes to her charity for hungry children."

"I don't know. I mean she can't be Esther Williams the old time move queen."

"The boy's father interjected, "Is Esther Williams.""

"The old time movie star?"

"Ol' but young."

"Well… all right. She is after all putting on quite a show."

"She is," Ethel said. "That swan dive from the high board – just so thrilling."

The boy's father spotted his son watching by the diving area exit ladder holding his mother's towel.

Mid-climb on the stairs to the third level, the star paused and waved to the crowd, and they waved and cheered.

"Isn't she lovely?"

"You can see her smile from here."

"That white bathing suit must have sequins, the way it sparkles."

"How I wish I had her legs."

"Exercise, honey."

"I exercise. I just don't have the result genes."

"There she goes," said Ethel. "Quiet now, Quiet everyone. Quiet."

The boy watched his mother far away on the third level, center her body then face the concrete platform over the water.

Her arms lifted, her legs strode, and half a length from the edge, she stiffened, pushed, and went soaring. As her back arched and arc-turned vertical, her feet and head twirled, and as the spear passed the second level, it twirled again, straightened, then disappeared like an icicle dropped into a pond.

The crowd cheered, and when their star broke surface and waved, they applauded until she climbed out and accepted the towel her son held to her.

"Thank you. Thank you," she called, then turned and asked her son in her native language, "Did you like that one, darling?"

"It was the best," he beamed.

"Oh, Miss Williams," said Ethel approaching the diving beauty. "Look how well we're doing for your charity." She showed the money inside a child's small bucket.

"Wonderful, Ethel." More?" she said turning to the crowd. "More?"

"Yes, Esther! More!" called a familiar man's voice in back. "From top!"

"Top?" she called. "Yes?"

"Yes!" cried the crowd.

"Oh my, she's diving from the tippy-top platform," Ethel fretted. "Come now everyone. Let's dig in and donate to Miss Williams' charity. She's diving all the way from the top for the children!"

People dropped coins and small bills into the passing bucket.

The boy's father, seated on one of the many concrete slabs that served as benches, saw his view of the performance obstructed as a man stepped in front of him. He moved to the side and spotted his wife skip up the second level stairs just as the man again covered his view. He craned his neck around the obstruction, got a clear view of his wife but only until the man shifted his weight.

"She's past the second level!" Ethel called.

The boy's father drew on his cigarette, bent over and set the red glow between the blocking man's bare feet.

"She's on her way to thre –"

"God damn!" yelled the man with the cigarette stuck to his sole.

The boy's father chortled just as the young man saw what stung him. "I don't believe it. You again!"

"Oh…" said the boy's father, his jaw slacking.

"You burn me again, funny man."

"Was mistake. I very sorry," he said turning serious.

"Mistake? Yeah. Sorry? Very."

Cheers from the crowd made them turn.

The showstopper waved atop the tower.

"Da! Da!" called the boy. "See her?"

"Come on, pops, you're coming with us."

Pointing to his mother, the boy turned again toward his father and saw him leave, the toughs cloaking him. The boy started toward the figures surrounding his father but stopped.

"Quiet! Quiet!" Ethel called.

He saw his mother approach the upper platform's edge, turn and only her toes grip land. He glanced back to the gang that swallowed his father, and though the bunch continued walking, his father reappeared from between them, kneeling forward on the ground.

"Da…"

"Oh my there she goes," he heard Ethel utter as he ran.

"Da. Da!"

His father slowly rose. "It's nothing," he said gaining his balance. "Did you see your mother's dive?" he asked holding his abdomen. "Give me her towel please."

The boy handed it, and when his father removed his hand to press the towel there, blood flowed.

"Don't be afraid. It's nothing. We needn't tell anyone."

"But Mommy."

"No, it's just a little cut. Let's not wreck her day. It'll stop bleeding and she'll never know. Go to her. Say the excitement of her performance made me so delirious I needed to sit. She'll laugh. Go."

The boy ran to poolside. The crowd applauded while his father passed behind.

"Oh Miss Williams!" Ethel cried. "So wonderful!"

"Thank you. Thank you!"

The boy's father crouched under the fence, then carefully lowered himself to the folding chair. When he removed the pressure from the wound, it bled. The knife's incision measured his thumb's width, and gapped above his appendectomy scar. That cut healed all right, he thought, and happened on a battlefield without hospital care. So would this. He only needed to stop the bleeding.

He reached into the satchel and pulled the belt from his slacks. As he did, he saw the two jetty fishermen head his way. Wishing to hide his trouble, he snatched his neatly folded shirt and slid it on. He spit on his hands and wiped the blood onto the towel he pressed against his wound.

One fisherman held a rod in one hand and in the other a third filled whisky bottle by the neck. His companion carried a rod and heavy looking bucket.

"Fish?" the boy's father motioned to the bucket.

"Eels."

"Eels...?"

"Eels." The bucket holding man lowered it to show a black slithering mass.

"Oh. You eat?"

"We eat 'em."

"You finish?"

"Done."

"You sell you whiskey?"

"Take it. We had enough."

"Thank you. Thank you much."

"Enjoy."

"Enjoy eels."

"Will."

He unscrewed the cap and took a drink. He then lifted the towel, took another drink, clenched his teeth and poured along the wound. He breathed deeply, composed, then retrieved his undershirt from the satchel, soaked whisky on a spot and applied it over the opening. He wrapped the towel around his waist and secured it with his belt. With a little more whisky he wiped his bloodied hands, then lowered his shirt over the bulky dressing. A quarter bottle remaining, he leaned back in the chair and drank while watching the boats on the inlet and cars on a suspension bridge spanning the dark water.

*

Holding the upturned liquor bottle, he watched the last drop slide onto his tongue, then hid the bottle in the satchel. The pain less, his humor returned and he mused the episode would turn out all right; yet, he grinned, if he died there on the grounds of the country's largest swimming pool, and the newspapers reported his demise, might they not announce, "As former Hollywood bathing star performs for fans, husband (and brick maker) lie dying." He chuckled. "Husband of Esther Williams dies from loss of blood while former movie queen enchants adoring crowds," he pictured. Drifting to sleep, he heard his son call, then appear through the fence.

"Da, Da, look what Mommy made!" He set a child's bucket containing coins and bills on his father's lap. "Mommy says there's as much as you paid for that man's shirt."

"Your mother's some piece of work."

"She told people she was Esther Williams the famous star who dove from all the diving boards and cliffs and bridges and things in the movies, and some ladies believed her and become her fans and they got all the people to give money for Mommy's charity while she put on a high dive show for them. You know how she does that funny pose with her arms out? She did that and said she was who she said she was as if she really was! It was so funny. How is your cut, Da? Did it stop bleeding?"

"It's fine."

"Mommy is still signing autographs but says you should come and we can go to the pool restaurant to eat whatever we want. There are rides there too and games."

"Tell your mother you both go. I'm tired from all the excitement, and I'm enjoying resting here watching the boats on the water. She'll understand. Just don't tell her about the cut."

"All right. I mean, I won't. And we'll bring you back something."

"Cold to drink."

"Bye, Da," he kissed his father. "Oh. I have to take the money bucket back. Mommy says she's challenging everybody to a swim race. Best out of ten races wins."

"Bring back the trophy tell her."

"Bye, Da."

His father closed his eyes and soon saw himself on a battlefield operating table, explosions all around, an army surgeon at his side snipping and removing his appendix.

Complaining to the doctor of deep pain in his abdomen, the doctor told him that the camp's anesthetic was old and useless, and he had no choice but do without.

"Remove your fists from inside my body then," he heard himself say to the surgeon, but the doctor held up and showed him his hands.

The doctor then reached a pair of tongs into a bucket and pulled out a wreathing black eel. Using it like a needle, he threaded it along the incision. With a second eel, he repeated the procedure in the opposite direction, stitching the wound tight, the eels still alive, mouths opening and closing, tails twisting.

"Sleepy head... Sleepy head..." he faintly heard a voice repeat. "Wake up, sleepy head."

His eyes opened and read the words formed perfectly on his wife's lips.

"Wake up my tired sleepy boy," she smiled kneeling next to him.

"Am I alive?" he asked.

She laughed. "Are you? Quite alive. As am I. As we all are on this lucky day."

"Where's the boy?" he asked holding his side.

"I'm here, Da," said his son seated behind his mother on the blanket.

"Did you rest?" she asked.

"Yes."

"Da, look how much money Mommy made."

He saw it packed in the small bucket.

"Mommy challenged everybody to a swimming contest across the racing pool. Best of ten races. And she won!

"Mommy's a champion."

"It only took three wins," she said smiling.

"They didn't have your stamina."

"No, they didn't know how to play the odds," she smiled.

"It pays to know how to bet."

"And keep your head."

"You're my champion," he said.

"Truly?"

"Always."

She turned, leaned back onto his chest, and he winced. "Something wrong?" she looked up.

"Nothing. I'm just... pleased."

"It's become a perfect day after all."

"Apparently."

She gazed at him, and he forced a smile.

"Let's top off this perfect day with ice cream," he said.

"The soft kind!" said his son.

"Any kind you want."

"We have plenty of money now," the boy said.

"Then let's get up and go," he responded. "The afternoon's almost over anyway. Come on. Up," he gently nudged his wife's weight off his side.

"Did you hear?" she asked him. "Some youths knifed a man."

"An ambulance took him to the hospital," his son added.

"I'm glad you didn't argue with that character about his shirt," she said. "With that bunch, who knows, they might have done the same to you. Wise to not tempt fate."

"You and the boy take the things and go ahead, and here, the car keys. Open it up to cool. The sun got me a little dizzy and I want to stop at the showers and cool off. I'll catch up."

"All right. We'll be at the car," she said. "Please don't forget to push back the fence."

The boy and his mother carried their bundles. His father waited, then passed under the fence, and upon losing sight of them, held his side and sat on a concrete bench. In that way, stopping at each bench, he traveled the municipal complex to the dank shade of the concourse.

He stopped at a water fountain. A line of people formed behind him by the time he finished drinking; but watered and shaded, his strength returned.

At the turnstiles milled many police officers, and standing at the near edge of the endless parking lot stood his son. "Mommy said I should wait for you."

"Why all the police?"

"I heard one say they're looking for the youths who stabbed the man the ambulance took. They're some sort of gang."

"Let's go."

"Is your cut all better?"

"All better."

They walked along a lane of the vast lot.

"Mommy said you were sad because you probably remembered going to a similar inlet with your family where you grew up; going there fishing with your brothers, and watching the boats."

"And catching eels?"

"That's what she said."

"She's right, and I might have; but I thought instead about this good day."

A clanging noise beside a parked car caught their attention. The boy's father paused and saw the iron crowbar from a tire change kit tossed from under a parked car. An arm appeared from under the vehicle, followed by its body. The man clutched the iron, crouched, and looked around. When he spotted the boy and his father, he thumbed they get lost.

As his father approached the youth, the boy recognized the young man.

"Go to your mother and wait," his father instructed.

The boy obeyed, and as he did, heard his mother whisper as if from a cloud, "Wake up, sleepy head.

Wake up, my sleepy boy," but kept walking without looking back.

"Stop right there, pops, or maybe you want some more ventilation," the young thug said.

The large approaching man did not slow.

"I'm telling you man, stop."

The thug brought back the iron and swung at the determined face, but the boy's father grabbed the arm, twisted it behind the youth's back, and with his free hand pulled the tire iron from the tough's fist.

"My boys are all around here, man. One call and they'll be all over you, and your kid."

"Call. Maybe come police too. Call."

"What you want, man? Just let me go."

The boy's father turned him around and pushed the chisel end of the iron rod between the thug's ribs.

"Man, that hurts!"

"Hurt? An' this?" he asked, pointing to his own midsection. "No hurt?"

"You burned me, man, and my shirt."

"An' I pay, no?"

"My wallet's in my back pocket, man," and he slid it out.

"How much you think cost my hole?"

"I don't know, man. Take a hundred."

"Oh, no. Is no how we do. You no remember?"

The youth held open the wallet, and the boy's father slid his fingers into the fold, pressed, and pulled out the batch of bills.

"Man, that's all our cash! That's over five – augh!" The iron tip jabbed his ribs. "Auagh, man. Take it. Take the money."

"An' I take this too," he said, taking the youth's driver's license.

"Take it man. Just get lost."

"An' keys," he said, opening his hand.

"Here," the youth said smacking them to the man's hand, which he then sent aloft to land between cars in another lane.

"Ohh man…"

"Now you go to keys an' you stay from me. Yes?"

He pushed the iron rod.

"Uuaa. Yeah man. Yeah!"

The boy's father turned and walked in his son's direction, then bent to toss the crowbar under a car. When he stood, he lurched, pinned his arms stiffly against a car trunk, concentrated on his trembling limbs until one gave, and still holding on with the other, saw gush from his mouth everything in his stomach. He choked, gasped, and his face burned hot as the car's metal.

He remained bent over the car until slowly, deep breathes returned. With his shirttails, he wiped his lips and chin. He checked the towel over his wound. Dry. He swallowed, straightened, faltered, then wobbling, staggered toward his car.

At the car, beside the driver's side door, he rested his arms on the roof and composed his shallow breathing.

His father remaining there, the boy peeked through the rear window, and when his father turned his way, for an instant the boy glimpsed the face of Christ, blood coursing over soiled clots, eternal thorns. Startled, his back dug back into the car's rear seat.

His father opened the door. The impression vanished.

"It's cooled off nicely," his wife said as he sat.

"Humm...?"

"The car. It cooled off like you wanted."

"Yes."

The engine turned over.

In the rear view mirror, the boy saw his father's eyes sullen, distant.

His mother tied her hair in a bun, closed her eyes and leaned back. "What a perfect day," she said. A breeze wisped through her window. "What a really happy day. No, husband?" And as she extended her hand to his arm, his head rolled to the side, his mouth gaped, and out the open mouth slithered two eels' heads.

"Wake up… Wake up sleepy head…wake up," the boy heard through haze. "Wake up, my sleepy head. My sleepy little boy."

The boy's eyes opened. They saw his mother. She wore a white bathing suit, the straps tied in a bow behind her neck.

"Have you forgotten, my sleepy boy? It's our day to visit the big pool."

Seated on the edge of his bed, she leaned over.

"Is Da alive?"

"Da is here," she smiled.

"You want me to croak already?" he teased, standing next to his mother.

"Da shouldn't smoke," the boy said.

"You're right. And he won't today at the pool. All right?"

"I'll suck a lollipop," his father smiled.

Gradually the boy lost his sleep, and placed his chin on his mother's shoulder, his head against hers. Against his hair he felt his father's great mitt, then heard his mother breath, "Today will be," and with her said, "a really happy day."

The Test

The boy knelt on the subway car bench gazing through the window at the distant buildings the train snaked toward. "Remember," said his mother seated beside him, "whatever you see today, tell no one."

He wasn't supposed to be there, not part of the plan to visit the government agency. But before he arrived at his aunt's after school, his cousin fell from her highchair, and his aunt rushed her to the hospital. The neighbor who otherwise sat for him, being away when his mother called, his mother hurried him to the subway saying he'd just have to come.

Up the line at an elevated station, his father boarded. He saw his son, lifted disapproving eyes at his wife, and sat opposite them in the long car, uncurling the Automobile Operator Regulations Manual from his fist.

Each stop of the way a deepening mound of laborers plodded into the car. They looked gloomy as his father, thought the boy. Their arms reached across his mother and him to brace against the wall. Hovering inches above them, their faces perched on forearms hanging from leather straps; yet, thought the boy, they wilted not a petal on his smiling just-like-on-TV "daisy fresh" commercials mom. Was that a meadow breeze blowing her hair?

As the swaying car jostled passengers side to side, through slits in the mass, the boy glimpsed his father bent over the automobile regulations manual, his forefinger dragged over sentences. Once, he pressed his finger to his lips, paused long, then shook his head.

For weeks, months, his father studied that automobile operator's manual filled with laws and rules of the road. Hundreds of words his father asked he translate from their native language to their adopted country's, looked like they now exploded in his father's brain. Many words his father asked him, he did not know, and he searched for them in the dictionary he bought with money he earned running errands for their next-door neighbor, Mrs. Klay.

Some words even his "Unabridged Dictionary" did not have, and his father would say, "How can the government expect a person to pass a test with words that even people from here won't know?"

But his mother kept saying he just had to study, and he would pass. And just in case, she had commended his case to St. Jude, patron saint of desperate causes, for a way through what his father called "a wilderness of words too great to conquer."

"A way will appear," she'd say. "Keep studying," she'd add while preparing his dinner in between his daytime job as a hauler at a brick factory, and night shift stacking bags at a flower mill.

Ever since his father's friend told them of a job, "a union job" his mother called it, "in the suburbs," his mother spoke of nothing but the job that could be theirs that paid twice what his father earned at his two jobs. It was their "great opportunity" and the way to own a house in "the suburbs," where everything was better.

Whenever she spoke of this house, her eyes "lit up," the boy's aunt said, as if she saw a golden apple sun rise beyond the shore of the beach they'd grown up near, when they still had everything and nothing had yet been lost. In this job that his aunt said his mother was determined to claim, she'd found the aroma of a blossoming lost pear orchard from back home. And the only thing missing to make the dream real, the boy's mother claimed, was a driver's license – a paper, a form, a nothing – for her husband. "What's a driver's license?" she'd say to the boy's father. "Nothing. You already know how to drive."

"I know how to drive, and well," he'd answer. "I drove bigger rigs than cars here. Trucks, artillery haulers, mule trains too, if they want to know. But what's it matter. To get to this job I need a license from here. From here. And I don't have one, and I can't pass a test with questions in a language I can't read."

"You'll study the manual. You'll memorize the words. Your son will help you. And you'll see it will all turn out in our favor."

"You always…"

"You'll see."

"I don't know."

"You'll see, you'll see."

"You think?"

"You can't lose this opportunity. Prepare, and a way will appear. It will. You'll see."

At the big station at city center, where one mass of travelers replaced another, huddled within the labor fragrant, the boy heard his parents finally greet. "Why is he here?" his father asked.

"Christa fell, and my sister rushed her to the hospital. She's fine; but anyway, the neighbor was out and I had no time. He'll just sit."

"This scheme of yours has me sick."

She turned to her son, "You're going to sit and just be quiet, right my darling?"

"Yes, Mommy."

Nearing the end of the stairs from under ground to the street, the boy watched his father's shoulders, like a giant bird's whose plumage had been compressed, expand to their regal size. Immediately he pulled out a pack of cigarettes, tapped it, and pulled a single with his lips.

"The place is, let's see, there, on the far side of the plaza," the boy's mother pointed.

"You always get your way, don't you," his father said dragging on the smoke and exhaling none of it.

"Come dear," she prompted her son across the city's grandest plaza.

The surrounding buildings with their long stepped approaches and high stone columns, the boy thought, looked like the ones Hercules walked through in the Roman times movies on TV he liked.

"I don't know if I can agree to this plan of yours," his father said as they walked. "I don't like it."

"Then don't do it, if you think you'll pass the test without it."

"It's cheating."

"Men do more than a little of that to get ahead. At least the ones I've heard about. And heard about, because they succeeded."

"By cheating."

"What did your friend do to get his big job?"

"He was compromised."

She laughed. "All right, let's call it that. And now he's in a position to help his friend. You. Is that so bad? Who does this hurt? No one. And help? All of us. Really. Does anyone get hurt?"

"Let it go."

"After all, you already know how to drive. That's what matters."

"What matters is a license."

"To get to the union job. And get our own house. And get away from slaving in factories. A little cheating can take a man far."

"Please. In front of the boy. You really have no conscience." He turned from their heading.

"Stay here," she said to her son and walked after her husband, but the boy could still hear.

"Are you afraid you can't do the job your friend's holding for you?"

"I can do the job," he answered flicking the cigarette butt.

"That we'll get caught? Arrested? Jail?"

"I've know jails," he sniffed.

"Then what?"

"Why does it seem we need to cheat to get ahead?"

"Because we don't have time to play saint. The reward is big and this is a small thing. Husband," she tugged his thick arm.

Staring at his shoes, he shook his head.

"It's only a moment," she said, "and you'll forget it. It's good for us. For you. For the boy. It's good."

He kept looking down.

"Try at least. If you can pass without me, then do. If you don't want my help, then just don't look my way – and then go ahead, and fail. And with every 70-pound sack of flower you lift tonight, you can embolden yourself for the next bag with the pride that you're a completely honest man, pure as the flower dust all over your face, back and hair."

*

At the testing area, the marble wall with many teller windows reminded the boy of the bank where he kept his Christmas Account. From a wooden bench along the hall's side, he watched his parents turn from different teller windows. His mother also carried a driver's test.

She surveyed the writing chairs in the testing area, then walked to an empty one next to a man wearing a black suit, red tie and a white handkerchief in his breast pocket, and she sat. His father followed and took a seat two chairs behind her in the same row.

A door in the marble wall opened and a woman with glasses hanging from a string around her neck, spoke to the test takers. "You'll have twenty minutes to complete this test. It's twenty multiple choice and comes all from the automobile operator's manual, so if you studied your manual, it will be easy. If not, see you at the re-take. Cheating –"

The boy's hands grabbed the edge of the bench.

"Cheating is prohibited and against the law. Anyone caught cheating, automatically fails, is barred from a re-take for 12-months, and subject to a fine and possible police prosecution."

The boy observed his mother smile her glorious smile at the test proctor the whole while, and wondered if she understood anything the woman said.

"You may begin…now. Turn over your answer sheet, and good luck."

The boy watched the test takers turn over their papers, his parents following their lead.

Everyone seemed to write their names at the top of their sheets. His parents looked about and did same. His father stared at his sheet, pushing his finger left to right over the page.

Except for coughs and the sound of crackling leather from one man's jacket each time he moved, the test area remained hush.

The boy noticed his mother constantly adjust her hair bun since the test began. He noticed his father watch the back of her head a moment, then look down and make a mark with his pencil on the answer sheet. He'd look up again and watch her head where her left hand beat spread fingers against her bun and her right hand held out one, two, three or four fingers.

The boy also perceived that before his mother adjusted her hair bun and made the sign language that looked like Indian's used on TV, she looked away from the well dressed man beside her.

"Five minutes," the proctor announced. The man next to his mother stood and walked with his sheet to a clerk window. His mother's left hand tapped five fingers four times against the back of her head, his father observing, and her right hand held out three fingers. She then stood and walked to a window, handed the clerk her test, and motioned her son to come.

As the boy passed the window next to his mother's where the man who sat next to her stood, he heard the clerk say, "Congratulations on passing the written portion. Only one wrong. Here's your learner's permit to prepare for the driving test."

The boy looked at his mother who he could see understood from the man's smile he had passed, and she smiled to her son and squeezed him to her side.

"I'm sorry, Miss.," said his mother's clerk, "you didn't pass." And the boy could see that from the clerk's expression his mother understood the verdict as well.

"Is all right," she smiled. "Thank you," she said and left.

"Do you want to reschedule? Miss, you can reschedule…"

His mother looked back and smiled, placed her arm on her son's shoulder, and continued along the wall of clerks.

Opposite the roped off testing area, she turned but her smile did not find her husband in the hall nor at any of the windows. Darting around, her smile lapsed only a second until she spotted him standing just before the stately building's exit.

"Congratulations," she exalted in their native language, and the boy saw her high heals go tippy-toe in order to reach and kiss his father. But as her heals lowered back to the marble, his father's head stiff, she responded, "You didn't pass. Tell me I'm crazy. You didn't pass."

His father looked away.

"But you couldn't fail. He passed. We saw he passed."

"Let's go," he said.

"He passed. Did you get mixed up? Did you mix up? Answer me."

"I didn't hand it in."

"You... You didn't hand it in?"

"I couldn't. Let's just go."

"Where's the test? The test. Where's the test!"

"Mommy, said the boy, his mother causing people to look.

"Where is it?"

The boy's father started out through the glass doors.

"The test!" His mother pulled his father's shirt and reached into a trouser pocket. "The test. It's mine. Give it to me. The test is mine. Give it."

"Check the trash," he snarled, pulled away, and left.

She hurried to the covered receptacle, pushed the swivel lid, but her reaching hand froze.

From the glass doors, the boy watched her small back. On the wide sidewalk, his father blew cigarette smoke.

She slid a tissue from her purse, passed it along her cheeks, pushed the swivel lid, dropped the tissue, then turned around and walked to her son.

"Mommy's all right, dear," she said in a faint voice, and she approached the doors, and he opened and held one for her.

"Thank you, my sweet."

Carefully she stepped down the slate steps to the sidewalk where his father stood. "I'm going to the factory," she said to him barely audible and looking away. "You'll take the boy home?"

He nodded.

"It's only to make up the time from leaving early. I'll return in time to prepare dinner before you leave for the mill."

He nodded again.

"My pretty," she bent to the boy, her eyes twitching. "Do your homework until Mommy gets back," and she held her cheek to his.

At the corner, when the light turned green, she crossed.

The boy's father cleared his throat looking at the imposing motor vehicle administration building they left, then turned around and exhaled. Behind them on the sidewalk stood a hot dog cart. Steam rose from the well as the vendor lifted the lid and stabbed a frankfurter for a customer.

"You want one?" the boy's father asked.

The boy's eyes sparkled. "But Mommy."

"We needn't tell her. Do you want one?"

The boy nodded quickly.

They approached the cart and his father pointed to the aluminum well and held up a finger."

"Mustard? the vendor asked.

The boy nodded.

The vendor held the filled bun to him on wax paper.

His father paid and they retraced their way to the subway station.

The boy kept the smell from the vendor's well in the bridge of his nose, and bit small pieces from the hot dog and bun. Sometimes he licked the mustard swirl, it stung, and then he bit the fluffy white bun.

His father stopped. They faced the front of a bar. Flashing green and red letters said Mac-something Tavern. Bottles of beer lined the sill of a narrow window.

"I'll bet you're still hungry," his father said. "Here they have better sausages than that."

As soon as his father pushed open the door to the dimly lit tavern, the smell of a cellar in an old building the boy once entered with his uncle to buy cured ham, filled his head. From the rear of the room came the crack of striking pool balls. That being the only noise, he heard his shoes scrape the sawdust on the wood floor as they walked to the long counter.

"No outside food," said the large man with rolled up sleeves behind the counter, aiming his chin at the last of the boy's hot dog.

His father stared at the man, then turned his head to his son as the boy filled his mouth with the snack's end. "Whiskey," his father said to the man.

"Kid's gotta have somethin'," the man said aiming his chin at the boy.

"What do you want to drink," the boy's father asked in their language.

The boy shook his head.

"You want that drink you like?" his father asked. "You're with me, not Mommy."

"Coke," the boy said to the bartender.

"Coke it is."

"And look," his father pointed, "there, in that server, they have sausages. Steaming. You can take one, in a bun, with sauce if you want."

The bartender smacked the glass of Coke on the counter, and the bubbles exploded over the surface. The boy's father handed his son the glass and the boy walked with it to the sausage cart.

"Chaser with that?" asked the barman.

"Beer."

When the boy returned with a sausage in a bun and his still untouched soda, his father was being poured another of the first drinks he ordered, and the barman took a bill from the pile on the counter next to his father's beer glass.

"Like the sausage," asked the barman.

"Yes."

"Ain't you gonna' drink your soda?"

The boy sipped and tasted it. This was maybe the best place he'd ever been, he thought.

He set his glass on a brick-red stool with brass nail heads around the edge. His father exhaled a long plume of smoke, and looked happy to the boy.

From behind a dark green curtain that gleamed like the material of the velvet jacket his mother bought him as a very special Easter present, a lady entered the room. She smiled, wore red lipstick like his mother, but the red dress and red high-healed shoes, his mother never wore. "A lady does not wear red," his mother said. And along the side of the lady's dress, a tear traveled up her leg. His mother was careful never to wear a dress with even a fray. She asked his father to buy her a drink, and he did.

"Another Coke?" the bartender asked him, and the boy accepted the fresh glass fizzing with his favorite although forbidden beverage. This really was the best place he had ever been, he thought as he stabbed another sausage.

*

By the third, or was it fourth soda and sausage, the boy sat in a battered rolling chair beside the pool table. The crack of striking pool balls woke him. His father tossed his cue on the felt, counted money in his hands, and handed the cash to one of the two other players.

"Better luck next time," said the man whose face the boy could not see because he stood behind the bright light bulb over the table.

His father no longer looked happy. He walked to the bartender, and when this one lifted the tall bottle to pour into his father's glass, his father covered the glass with his hand and shook his head. With the lady, he took several steps, pushed aside the luxurious curtain, and disappeared.

The boy then turned his head and examined his empty soda glass and the butt of his last sausage and bun, then turned back, and beside him unexpectedly saw his father. "It's time to leave," he said.

"To Mommy?"

"Yes."

"Take it easy," a pool player said to his father as the boy and he turned from the table.

"Take easy," his father answered.

"Thanks for nothing, buster," said the lady, as they passed the counter.

"Take easy," his father replied.

It was almost dark outside, and dark when they walked up the front steps of their row house.

His mother in the kitchen when they entered, had not changed clothes, and fake strands of hair from the factory where she sewed these into rubber doll heads, glistened on her sweater. The table was set on a fresh white tablecloth, and she wore the scent his father liked.

"Wash your hands and sit. I'm just heating last night's, and it's ready.

His father ambled to the sink. He washed his hands, splashed water on his face and tucked his shirt.

"Enjoy yourself with Da?"

"Yes."

"He knows lots of good places."

His father's shoulders sloped and he avoided getting in his mother's way as she scooted from table to stove to frig.

When his father sat, she brought him his gallon wine jug. "I know you like it chilled, so I cooled it in the frig. But you pour. It's too heavy for me."

He poured while looking at a wallet size card prominently leaning against his glass.

When the boy's mother sat, she said, "I think I'll have some wine too tonight," and her husband poured her half a glass. She claimed that because she was little, she could not drink a lot.

"A toast," she said, lifting her glass.

The boy's father lifted his, and the card leaning against it dropped. The boy lifted his milk and they clinked glasses. "To our future," she said.

His father set his glass on the card.

"It's not a coaster," she smiled.

"Whatever it is," he said, "if it's from you it's trouble."

"Well, Mr. Pessimist, it's from Dad Klay."

His father lowered his fork and picked up the card from their next-door neighbor who was always kind to them and had sold him his old car with the Indian chief on the hood.

"It's a way to drive the car he sold you until you get your license," she said. "Isn't it wonderful!"

The boy's father turned the card over, then reached it to his son. "What does it say?"

"Honorary Officer," his wife answered looking intently at her son's eyes as she said it.

"Is that what is says?" his father asked him about the words above the gold embossed five point star.

Unsure if the words also meant Honorary Officer, his mother's flame flickering eyes heating his face, he answered, "Yes, Da."

His mother smiled, took the card and handed it back to her husband. "What luck to meet Dad Klay on returning home," she said. "He saw I looked sad, and through my sister – we coincided on her way back from the hospital – I explained to Dad about your job opportunity, and he pulls this card out of his wallet. Go ahead and drive the car you bought from him, and if the police stop you, which they won't because you're an excellent driver, but if they do, you show them this card and they'll let you go. It's a special card a retired police officer like Dad gets. Forty-one years on the force, you know. But don't say anything about it to anybody. It's a very special badge only he's privileged use of, so not a mention. Honorary Officer. Put it in your wallet and keep it there."

"I can go ahead and drive?"

"Like with a real license."

The boy observed his father's hunched back start to uncurl.

"Are you sure?"

"Positive."

"I'm still going to retake the written test though," he said sliding the card into his wallet.

"Of course. This is temporary until you get your own. But in the meantime…" Her eyes widened smiling at the wallet.

"And after the written, I can take the actual driving part."

"Which you'll pass on the first try because you're an excellent driver."

"And that car Dad Klay sold me," he said, his fork stabbing a large cube of meat, "it's old but drives so smooth. Turns like with only one hand on the wheel. Marvelous automobile – which I'm going to make even better; clean the carburetor, tune the plugs, change the belts, retread the tires. You'll see, when we drive in that car... You'll see. Like in a limousine. Like your father owned."

"Wait 'till they see us. In our car. Shinny the way you'll get it. And the old leather, I'm going to buff, clean and make soft. How it'll glow!"

"What luck."

"You'll call your friend later and tell him to ready your job start, and you prepare whatever you need to."

"Pay the money to join the union, drive to work, and it's done."

His father, gobbling food so fast, swallowing glassfuls, the boy thought he must have missed lunch – and breakfast!

"You're sure that's what Dad said?"

"Yes. My sister was there. You can ask her."

"Honorary Officer," he said, the side of his finger passing under his moustache. "Thank you," he leaned to her to share a kiss. "But be careful," he turned, "anybody around misbehaves, I'll arrest them."

"Not I," she laughed. "I'm a good girl."

The boy could not eat, even losing his appetite for the rare, store bought strawberry short cake his mother purchased.

*

The boy's father began the union job. He was still away most of the time but the boy's mother told the boy that when they moved closer to his father's work in the suburbs, his father would be home sooner and they'd travel to many beautiful places together.

And during this time, his mother acted like his friends did while waiting for the presents they wanted for their birthdays. She talked every day about their future home and the schools he would attend and things they'd do after she saved enough, thirty-four months from then, to buy their modern new home.

*

When the boy next saw his father's officer badge, thirty months away from getting their new home, it was at school. Show And Tell Day. A classmate came dressed as a police officer because that is what he was going to be.

The classmate wore a police hat, and carried handcuffs on his belt, and taped to his blue dress shirt pocket, shone a card with a five point gold embossed star. The

Junior Officer told the boy that it came in a box of oatmeal cereal. Junior Officer is what he was. It said so above the gold star on the card – just as the boy remembered.

The card meant his classmate could arrest people if they broke any rules. Was he allowed to drive a car with it, the boy asked.

*

Month twenty-nine or twenty-eight away from their new home, on his fourth or fifth try, the boy's father passed the written part of the driver's test and received a learner's permit, which his wife framed and stood on a radiator cover until the winter months arrived.

His father failed the driving test the first time because the tester said "right" and his father turned right when what the tester meant was "correct."

The retake, month twenty-five away from their new home, was scheduled for Christmas Eve. His father was sure he would pass, and immediately afterward, unlike previous years when the boy and he walked the many blocks to buy their Christmas tree, they'd drive to the tree sellers. And the tree seller would place the tree on the roof of their car, and secure it with twine.

Christmas Eve, snow started early afternoon. The boy's mother, worried they cancelled the driving test, did something she never did; she called his father at work. Even as the skies darkened and snow closed roadways, his father said he would go to the testing place.

To celebrate their hero's triumph, the boy's mother baked his father's favorite savory treat, almond cakes. She made them this time with extra care, even making the paste filling herself, and asking her sister to lend her expertise so they'd taste as close as possible to the ones from their country.

As night fell, his mother had the table set with candles, treats, and special wine. She removed her apron and revealed her new dress with ruffles and a bow for a buckle, and of course, matching new high heals.

They unwrapped and placed the perfect Baby Jesus porcelain figure from their country into its twig crib with golden straw. Ready to place it under the coming Christmas tree, they heard the bolt on the front door, snap.

"Da," the boy said, and he ran to the kitchen.

His father entered covered white. He marched slowly in step, stamped the snow from his shoes, and brushed the frost from his coat, and the boy's mother, who came up behind her son, did not rebuke his father about the mess as she normally would.

Instead, she went to him silently, bent, and untied his shoelaces, removed his wet shoes, and slid his slippers under his feet, then took his coat to hang from the bar in the bathroom over the tub.

His father sat at the table and poured a glass from his jug. "Test was cancelled."

His wife nodded and lowered her eyes. "What else happened?" she asked, the edges of her mouth quivering.

"I skidded at a stop sign, drove through it, and nipped a parked car's bumper."

"And…?"

"And a police car stopped me."

"And…?"

"And I showed my card."

"And…?"

"And he didn't recognize it. Except to say you and his wife buy the same oatmeal."

"Oh…"

"The cop spoke a little of our language and suggested that the owner of the car I hit might live in the house, and that he'd wait 'till I settled the damages. I did. And being Christmas Eve, he said he wouldn't fine me, but impounded the car because, well because I didn't have a license to operate it. Did I?"

Still looking down, his wife shook her head slowly.

He took a sip from his glass.

"Good man, that cop," he continued, "Reminded me of my middle brother. The eyes. I tipped him and he took it. It's Christmas after all."

She looked up, her head to one side.

"I'm not angry. You meant well. I'm a lucky man. We'll get the car back, and I'll schedule another test, and another, and many as necessary, and I'll pass, and we'll get your house, and everything you dream. Tonight only means it'll take a little longer, at the mill, the factory. A little longer. That's all it means. That all right with you?"

She took his hand, turned it, and touched her lips to the palm. And he took hers, held it to his heart and brought his lips to the bend of her fingers. Then he asked his son, "What time do the tree sellers close, do you think?

"Ten, the sign says."

"I think we can make if before then. But wear your boots. Snow's already high, and folks don't shovel their walks Christmas Eve."

"And this time, can Mommy come?"

"No," she answered, "it's for you two."

"Then let's enjoy your mother's fine meal," his father said. "We'll need our strength to make it there, and back."

Last Day At The Beach

The first shark the boy saw attack his mother, darted away distracted, but now high above him at the surface, seven black beasts circled her. Her arms splashed, and her legs dangled like Christmas tree ornaments on a low branch. From below, he saw the biggest shark's open mouth lunge for her punching arm, and then as if through water-plugged ears, he heard his mother's soft voice: "We have to be back from the beach before the church doors close."

His eyes opened.

"Were you asleep, my darling?"

"No. Yes," he answered sitting next to her.

"Today's Grand-Da's anniversary. Two years gone. We have to light a candle after the beach."

The train jolted and tossed the boy against its metal side.

"Oh this train," his mother reacted in her native language, the passengers seated in the facing row, looking away slowly.

"Mommy?" the boy asked.

"Yes, darling?"

"When you swim far out at the beach, do you see sharks?"

"Of course," she smiled.

"Aren't you afraid?"

"I? Your mother afraid? Of course not."

"Aren't you afraid one will eat you?"

"They wouldn't dare."

"What if one tried?"

"If a shark misbehaved? I'd reach out my arm and punch it in the snout, and it and all the other sharks would scatter like puppies."

The boy laughed and huddled against her.

"But you needn't worry about sharks. They don't bother anyone where you play in the shallows."

"Mommy, even after I learn to swim well, I don't want to go where the sharks are. And don't you go there today yourself, all right?"

"All right, dear. Now nap if you want. It's still a way to the beach."

"I'm not tired," he said and turned to watch the elevated subway stations pass, and the brick and clapboard houses glowing warm yellow from the morning sun.

The trip from their city row house to the shore took hours and several train changes. Because his mother preserved her love of the beach, formed when she grew up near one in her country, she made the trek so he too "would come to love the beach and sea."

Once a week for five weeks they made the trip, using the five days vacation she received from the doll factory where she worked. She was the only mother from the neighborhood who troubled to make the trip, and because it took so long, they stayed all day.

The following mornings he told the boys on the street stories of his great adventure: hunting for starfish in the jetties and rotting piers, catching little silver fish in a net his mother sewed from worn stockings, his mother's fearlessness swimming beyond the breakers to the deep ocean – and the fear it caused the lifeguards (though it was he who became frightened).

Along the way, the elevated subway passed the botanical gardens, and he strained to spot the royal peacock strolling the shaded lawns. One time he saw it open its tail and walk into the sunlight, and when it fanned its rainbow, and the colors gleamed, his heart quivered as well, and his head felt light.

Farther along when he sighted the gray stone monument, "size of a pyramid" a passenger once said, angels and chariots on every level, he knew they'd soon change train. His mother said the monument honored the soldiers who died in a war, so that people would not forget them.

When the smell of what his mother called "the sea" wafted through the train car's open windows, he knew they neared the last change of trains. Along the remaining stops, "the smell from the sea," at the foot of the big city, strengthened, evoking the smell of the black tar streets he played on during a hot summer day.

On the elevated station's bridge after they arrived at their final stop, his mother paused and gazed at the far ocean. "Remember it," she sighed. "This is our last trip to the beach this summer." The long, rocking train trip had ended. The pricks on his tender under thighs from the splintered straw seats they sat on disappeared. The clanging metal beat departed his ears as his memory heard the steady crash of waves upon the shore.

"Take your bag, darling," she said, and they walked the three-story stairway to the street, where the apartment buildings shaded them until they stepped onto the boardwalk.

There they paused again while his mother gazed over the beach already teaming with so many people, that spotting unclaimed sand seemed difficult. "Aren't we fortunate?" she smiled. "Come on," she said crossing the splintered planks. And like Cinderella stepping from her horse drawn carriage onto a cushion, when her foot touched the sand, she cooed, "How lovely," just like every previous visit.

She then removed her thick cork heal sandals, slid them in her beach bag, and continued walking. "Come on, my boy. Stay close to Mommy and don't get lost," she warned.

They walked through a maze of blankets and chairs to the line fronting the white foam. There, "Where it's cooler," they stretched their blanket. There, his mother unveiled like a swan. She unbound like the onward angles upon the victory memorial to the heroes. Wearing the only black bathing suit on the beach, she scalloped her white rubber bathing cap over her billowing hair, and sprinted to the water.

"Mommy. You won't go far, you said!"

"Watch Mommy!" she smiled back.

"Mommy you said –"

"Watch me wave!"

He watched her dive into a breaker. "Mommy..."

When the boy saw his mother's bathing cap reappear, it was beyond half the breaking waves. He wanted to call out as he did other times his mother swam for the sea, but knew she could not hear.

Pawed by another wave, the white speck disappeared a long time before reemerging. On cue, a lifeguard whistle blew. One whistle, then three. His mother waved to the shore, to him he knew, even far as she was. And instead of heeding the lifeguard whistles, which blew louder than usual, she turned, and from her stroking arms the boy saw droplets of tinsel-like streams catch the sun.

Lifeguards from neighboring stations kept arriving at the tall lifeguard chair near the boy. All blew whistles and sounded so loud, the boy thought, his mother must hear. But when the guards on the high chair waved she return, she only waved back, and he imagined, flashed her pearly smile.

It seemed much longer than she ever ignored the lifeguards' call to return, he thought. Then he saw six lifeguards push the sleek lifeguard rowboat he thought only a decoration, never seeing it launched, and it slit the water before cresting the first breaker.

Police arrived. One was a woman officer, who stopped beside him, and who looked odd to him wearing so many clothes on the beach.

"Sharks," the boy heard a lifeguard say to the police.

"She drowning?" A cop asked the guard.

"No," said a guard standing on the lifeguard chair looking through binoculars. "Surrounded by sharks. Six, seven fins."

"Mommy!" called the boy. "Mommy, come!"

"That your mommy?" the policewoman asked.

"Yes."

The bathers and those on the sand watched the skiff's six rowers crash through waves toward the placid water where the still far swimmer no longer waved.

"She still, ah, all right?" a cop asked the lifeguard holding binoculars.

"Fighting."

"They gonna reach her in time?

"Don't know."

"I want you to come with me," said the policewoman, placing her hands on her knees and lowering her face to the boy. "We'll wait for your mommy in a nicer place," she smiled.

"I can't leave my mommy."

"Come with me, honey. Your mommy would want you to do what a police offer said. We'll go to a nice place and I'll bring her there in a little while. Come." She reached for his hand, and he took it. "Have some gum," she said handing him a stick. "Cinnamon. Ever try it?"

"No," he said looking over his shoulder walking with her and tasting the gum's spicy flavor.

"Good, isn't it?"

"Tickles."

"Does," she chuckled. "I think I'll have one too."

He walked without sandals and the sand burned, but when they arrived at the place, the side of a long concrete wall shaded the sand. The police officer approached a woman standing at the entrance of the bunker-like building.

"Boy lost mommy?" the woman asked the officer.

"Um, this one's not lost. Mommy will be by soon."

"What's all the commotion down there?"

"Nothing. Just a swimmer went a little far."

"Little far? Half way to China, with all that commotion. Half the beach crew there looks like. Shark attack?"

"No, no, everything's under control. Everything's fine," she said, the boy seeing her head flick in his direction.

"Of course. Everything's fine," the lady said. "Mommy'll be here before you know it. Thanks, Lorrie. I'll take him now. Say," she added, bending to the boy, "You want some gum?"

The edges of the boy's mouth tightened and turned down.

"Well, here's one for later," she said handing him a stick.

"I'll be back," the officer said to the woman.

"Bye. Hi to Paul. Well," she turned to the boy, "come on in," and she led him into a dark, concrete tunnel. "This is the lost children's place – even though you're not really lost. You'll stay here so you don't get lost, and so your mommy can find you. And that won't be long. So go on down with those children and sit. It's nice and cool back there."

"My mommy will come for me soon?"

"Real soon. Go ahead. They're nice kids. Your age. Go on."

The boy walked the tunnel's cold concrete floor to a slab where sat two boys and a girl about his age.

"Hey kid, got any gum?" The tall boy asked.

"I have this," the boy said reaching out his gum.

"Thanks," said the tall boy swiping it.

"My name is –" started the boy.

"We don't have names here, kid," the tall boy said sticking the gum in his mouth.

"This here's the land of lost boys," said the big round boy.

"And girls," said the girl.

"We ain't got no names," the big one added.

"Only a rendezvous with destiny," said the tall one. "You know how to play poker?"

"No."

"Well that's too bad, 'cause we do."

"I'm tired of playing cards," the girl said. "Let's play something else."

"Like?"

"Like if you had all the money in the world what would you buy?"

"Oh that's easy," said the big boy.

"Yeah, but it's got to be something not stupid," the tall boy said.

"I'd buy a solid gold car," said the big boy.

"See. That's what I mean. Stupid," the tall boy said.

"Why?"

"'Cause if it's solid gold, it's too heavy to drive, stupid."

"Not with a super deluxe motor, stupid. With super strong rocket ship things. Like a battle tank. Ever see ah army battle tank, dummy? They're heavy. Heavy as a house, and they move."

"Not fast, imbecile."

"Faster than your mother."

"Wait, wait, wait. Stop!" said the girl. "You're both stupid, because this is a suppose game, so it can't be stupid. Whatever you want, you can have. Anything. Even a solid gold car."

"See. Stupid," the big boy said.

"I," said the girl, placing her hand to her breast, "would buy a fairytale castle, on a mountain, surrounded by a forest with a shimmering, winding river. Little pink butterflies flutter in the magic woods, and my white unicorn with the blue eyes lives there and plays with me."

"And a big stupid prince takes you in his smelly arms and kisses you," the big boy said.

"And turns you into a frog," teased the tall one, and the two boys laughed.

"You're such childish stupid boys," she snapped. "What would you get?" she asked the tall boy.

"Me. I'd get an army. Of mercenaries."

"Of what?" asked the big boy.

"They're soldiers that you pay to kill everybody who ever was mean to you or hit you."

"Cool…" said the big boy.

"Then I'd tell 'em, build me a fort and kneel and bow to me and beg me to grant you mercy. And then I'd buy a —"

"I don't want to hear any more about what you'd buy," said the girl. "You got your thing, and you only get one. What about you?" she turned to the new boy. "What would you buy with all the money?"

"I would buy a magic lamp. Like in the movie."

"Oh yeah, I saw that! You get three wishes," the big boy said.

"What would you wish?" asked the girl.

"I would wish that my Mommy and Da always stay with me."

The children glanced away from him a moment, then back.

"That's only one, no, two wishes," the tall one said low. "Your dad, and your mom. Two. What about the third?"

"A driver's license for my Da. To make my mom happy."

"That's it?" asked the tall boy.

"When I get my driver's license," said the big boy, "I'm gonna get a convertible, for everybody to see, solid gold, and with a rocket engine and a parachute and those thumbtack squirting cannons and —"

"And I wish you'd just shut up," the tall boy interrupted.

"Oh yeah? Well make me."

"I'll make you. I'll punch you in the face."

"I'll kick you in the teeth."

"Poke your eyes in."

"Stupid idiot."

"Stupid donut brain."

The argument blurred then grew muffled to the boy. The cards to the card game they then played seemed to him big as a house, the coins, heavy as stones. And after his turn at blind man's bluff, he refused to open his eyes – until, "Looks like somebody's mom is here."

Sunlight behind his mother, the boy saw her outline at the tunnel's entrance appear like the church statue of The Blessed Virgin Mary. He slid off the concrete slab, and in an instant, his arms circled her waist.

"My angel," she whispered holding him.

"Did the sharks do that?" he asked about her arm in a sling. "When you punched them in the nose as they attacked you?"

"No, my dear boy. They didn't bother Mommy. A lifeguard's oar hit Mommy's arm by accident."

"Mommy," he hugged her. "Don't leave me ever again."

*

The rest of the day the boy's mother entered water only below her waist, helping her son find starfish in the jetties. They found only one and it may have been dead, but while police wrote his mother "a ticket," a boy offered him twenty-five cents for the starfish, and the boy traded it for the coin, sliding it into his bathing suit pocket.

After most people left the beach, they too gathered their belongings and headed to the boardwalk. There, unlike every other visit, his mother could not give him ten cents for an ice cream, her purse having vanished from her beach bag.

Walking to the train station, she said, "I have no money for fares. I'll have to come up with something, so whatever I say, you're to do it, all right my good boy?"

"Just don't leave me, Mommy."

They started up the three-story stairway to the elevated line.

As they approached the turnstiles, they passed a posted police officer. The boy's mother stopped in front of the turnstiles a moment, then bent to the boy. "Go ask the policeman which train goes north," she said.

The boy shook his head.

"I'll wait here."

His head shook and lips pressed.

"Do what I say, my boy."

"No," he chocked softly.

"I'll stay here. I promise."

"I'm not going from you."

"Darling, I don't have money for tokens. Do as I say. I'll wait right here."

The boy turned and walked to the police offer, who bent down and listened. After the boy received his answer, he turned again and saw his mother standing on the other side of the stiles. He turned and headed to the exit stairs. His mother called but he kept moving. She called until she could wait no longer, then crossed back to the entrance side, and stopped him on the steps just before the street. "Dear heart. Why did you disobey Mommy?"

"You didn't," he said gulping, "You didn't keep your promise. You didn't stay. You said you wouldn't swim far. And you said you wouldn't leave."

"My precious boy. I'm sorry. I'm very, very sorry. Precious boy." She brushed back the hair from his brow. She breathed deeply. "I promise we won't separate even for a second. We'll stay together. Don't cry"

"Do you promise?"

"I promise."

They held hands and walked to the street and the dozen blocks to the next station. They climbed the multi-story stairs and attempted to pass under the turnstiles together, but a passenger shouted to the token booth attendant, who waved them back.

The next station took another twelve blocks to reach. They tried again passing under the stiles, and two quick peeps from a police whistle returned them to the stairs.

Approaching the next farther seeming station, and climbing the long stairs, the boy remembered the twenty-five cents in his bathing suit.

His mother purchased a token. To save the boy's fare for what she needed later, she squeezed him through the stile with her but a token booth employee emptying tokens from the stiles stopped them.

She opened her son's mouth for the man, "Look baby teeth."

"I ain't buyin' no mule, lady, and he ain't no jackass. He's old enough to pay the fare; now buy one."

*

Sunset framed in their home station's elevated windows, the boy and his mother lumbered off their journey's final train and strode the last blocks home.

"I still have Grand-Da's candle to light," his mother sighed, her slung arm sagging, her beach bag tugging

128

her other shoulder, and, thought the boy, her face crumpled like a towel dropped on the floor. "It was a promise," she added.

"Is church still open?" he asked.

"Just a little longer. I can leave you with your aunt while I go."

"I'll come."

They forged past their row house and the half dozen streets to the church.

His mother knelt at a bank of votive candles, he beside her. She folded her hands and prayed, crossed herself, and he followed. From her beach bag she took her bathing cap, spread it open and retrieved the five-cent fare change from his twenty-five cent piece. "For the offering," she said handing him the coin. He slid it in the slot at the candles' base, and together their hands carried a flame atop a wax stick to a candle in memory of who had left.

An Order Of Chicken

The boy and his father stood gazing into the window of Two Brothers Delicatessen. Six roasted-brown chickens rotating on a spit oozed lustrous fat. The amber juice slid along their sides and dripped into an aluminum tray partly hidden by twisted hot-red cardboard flames. The lit orange sign above the rotisserie proclaimed "B-B-Q Chickens" as flickering red flames licked the letters.

"They look moist, don't they?" the boy's father asked in their native language.

"They're shiny."

"B... B... Q... she... she... she-ken," his father pronounced. "Let's buy one," he added, and placed his hand on his son's shoulder leading him to the deli's glass door.

"Won't Mommy mind?" the boy asked.

"Why should she? These are good chickens. Nothing artificial, no? Just a fresh chicken slid on a rack and cooked. What could she mind?"

She always did, thought the boy, about prepared foods. His mother claimed store bought foods, including hot dogs and hamburgers were "junk," full of "artificial ingredients" not good as what she bought fresh and prepared for them at home.

But this night's dinner his father would prepare, his mother staying at the hospital with her sister who earlier gave birth to his new cousin.

"B... B... Q... she-ken," he repeated. "Am I saying it right? he asked his son.

"I think so."

"B, B, Q, She-ken. Darn but we're going to dine on a delicious chicken tonight," he said leading them to the delicatessen.

While they waited in line before the tall, refrigerated deli counter, the boy's eyes surveyed the glass case of cold cuts, prepared garnishes and puddings. He often wondered how they tasted, and imagined they tasted special if people bought them. Tiny flags on toothpicks said each creation's name and price per pound. "Can we also get some potato salad, Da? Just to taste."

"You want potato salad?"

The boy smiled and nodded.

"Then you get potato salad. But don't tell Mommy you like it better than hers if she asks."

"It won't taste as good. And potato chips?"

"Grab a bag,"

"Next," said one of the two big countermen in long white coats surveying the customers.

"B B Q she-ken," said the boy's father proudly.

"What did you say?" the deli man answered.

"One," the boy's father said holding up his forefinger.

"Before that."

"B B Q she-ken. Sheken, one," the boy's father repeated.

"One… what?"

"B…B…Q… she-ken," he answered stressing each letter.

"Bill," the deli man turned to his partner, "can you understand what this guy's sayin'?"

"Not a word. If they're even words."

"She-ken. B B Q one."

"I heard that already, fella. But that don't mean you said anything. Why don't you go figure out what you want and how to say it and come back then. Who's next?"
"No. I."

"Buddy, speak the language or stop holding up my line. I got customers waitin'. Who's next?"

"I'm next," the man behind, signaled.

"No! I. B B Q sheken. You look," and he pointed at the front window. "Sheken. One. B B Q. Look light. Like is. B B Q."

"Mister. I got people waiting. Now say it right or say it somewheres else."

The boy's father held up an open hand like a policeman and turned to his son.

"Bob," said a customer, "for Christ's sake, the guy's pointing at the barbecue chickens in the window. He wants a chicken. Give 'em one damn it and let's go."

"Excuse me, Tom, but don't tell me how to run my counter. He'll tell me what he wants right or he can go. And I'm gettin' damn tired of him holding up my line."

"We want a barbecue chicken," the boy called hidden by the tall deli unit.

"Is that what you want, buddy?" the deli man asked the boy's father. "Huh? A barbecue chicken?"

"Yes," his head gestured.

"Please, you could at least say."

"Try and learn the lingo, mister" the other deli man added as his partner walked to the window display to slide a piece off the spit.

The boy watched his father stare ahead at the white tiled wall behind the tall counter, his gaze fixed like when he looked at bad grades on his report card. The boy no longer wanted the perfect dishes of fancy foods, and wished they'd stayed outside. He laid the potato chip bag back on its shelf, and saw his father notice, then slide a cigarette from his shirt pocket. His father's face changed from looking like he was lost and asking directions, to like when he played cards, covered them, and then bet all his money. And like then, he blew a cloud of cigarette smoke instead of exhaling none. "We don't need the potato salad," the boy said pulling his father's belt.

The counterman wrapped the chicken in foil, and plopped the white paper bag on the tall counter. "One barbecue. Next."

"An'," the boy's father said turning to his son, "ask for the salad."

"I don't want it."

"Ask."

"Potato salad."

"Uh boy," the deli man breathed. "Salad. How much?" "How much?" the boy asked his father.

"Pound."

"A pound," the boy called.

"And take the chips," his father said.

The boy reclaimed the bag.

"Pound of salad." Plop! "Next!"

The boy's father took the two white paper bags and turned with his son for the checkout. He handed the cashier the scribbled receipt, and she punched the numbers as the boy's father pulled on the last of his cigarette. Then, whereas he normally dropped the butt on the floor and snuffed it, the boy saw his hand move above a waste paper basket beside his leg, his fingers part, and the butt fall into the trash as his toe pushed the basket against a display of packaged pastries.

"Your change," said the cashier.

The boy's father nodded and he and the boy walked out the door.

There, the boy's father stopped and lit another cigarette, and when he exhaled, no smoke came out his mouth or nose. He then turned around, the boy following suit, and through the glass door, the boy saw flames tall as he dancing over the pastry display.

Customers stood far behind. The countermen shielded their eyes with one arm and with their other swatted the flames using their white deli coats.

The boy looked at his father. He smoked and watched as if nothing happened. He did not return to help as was right, thought the boy. And when customers finally ran out coughing and complaining, he did not move away from the door, forcing the customers to pass around.

When the countermen stopped smacking the flames, pastry packages littered the deli floor. Drawing quick breaths, their hands rested on their waists. When they glanced beyond the glass door to the street, the boy saw they spotted his father and him, and his father flicked his cigarette butt at the deli door. He then placed his hand on the boy's shoulder, turned him, and they walked away past the deli window.

"Hey!" the boy heard the muffled countermen yell.

"You! Hey! You! The men called behind them as he and his father walked up the city sidewalk.

"Come back here you! You ___!"

The words the boy heard, had he said them, he knew he'd need tell at Holy Confession.

"You! Damn! I'm calling you! You!

The obscenities grew distant.

"Da. They were calling us."

His father nodded and kept walking.

At the corner, the boy's father stopped and stared ahead as if waiting for the crossing signal, except the light shone green. His hand reached in his back pocket, then handed his son a clip of folded money. "Here. Return to the store and pay for the damages. The basket, shelves, and garbage your mother doesn't buy. Bring back the rest."

The boy nodded and turned back.

"I'll wait in here," his father said motioning to a store without windows or signs.

*

The boy handed one of the deli men the money clip and told him its purpose. The man counted it, said it was hardly enough, but slid it in his pocket and told the boy to "beat it back to your S.O.B. father," and that his old man better not show his face near there again.

When the boy hesitated and said his father told him to bring back change, the other man answered, "Sonny, you better get out-a-here before we hold you for ransom. Now move before I get my strap on you, and gun on your S.O.B. father. Get!"

*

The boy waited outside the store where his father left him. He smelled something like his mother's leather jacket, turned around, then realized it was his shirt. His eyes still itched from the smoke. When the store's door squeaked open, he stopped rubbing them. Behind the exiting man, he spotted his father sitting on a stool at a bar's end, laughing with a lady.

The boy caught the door before it shut, and entered.

The laughing lady leaned from behind the bar, holding his father's hand.

"This is my son," his father smiled as his son approached and his small eyes held his gaze.
"Handsome," she said in their native language. "Looks like dad. Do the girls say you're handsome?"

The boy's moist eyes, like a faithful, disillusioned dog's, lowered his father's.

"Does he look like his mom?" the woman asked her customer.

He nodded, his hand leaving hers, two fingers pulling on his moustache.

"Care for a drink, handsome?" she asked.

The boy's soft face held his father's tense grin.

"I think you can do with a drink," she smiled to the boy.

"Can we go home?" the boy stammered.

The man's grin shriveled. He reached to the boy, lifted and held him, and the boy heard a rubber heal swipe the linoleum floor, except the screech came from beside his ear, once, only once, just before his father exhaled beer or wine or something else.

A Trip To The Falls

The boy's grandmother sat still as a saint contemplating the Lord's creation. Serene in the back seat of his parents' car, she reposed as if the bench were made for her. It was that way whatever she occupied; a chair or couch, a sidewalk or room, beside a door or person, and when she left, the space felt like a missing tooth.

Before she arrived from his parent's country, he had seen her only once, when his mother took him over the ocean to see his grandfather. The whole visit, Grand-Da never left his bed in the big house. There, his mother fed him soup each afternoon, and he thanked her for her "kindness" and for bringing his grandson "before He takes me... Before He takes me." Afternoons in the kitchen, he remembered Grandma sang him horsy songs, bouncing him on her knee, laughing when he giggled "Faster, horsy, faster!"

She wore only black dresses now, and black stockings and shoes, her only color the gold medallion of The Blessed Virgin With Savior, and her many gold teeth.

His grandmother wished to visit the great falls she had seen in pictures and that his parents hoped to see since arriving in their new country. Maybe seeing them would make her happy again, the boy thought. Now, she just sat, and smiled.

"How are you both holding up back there?" the boy's father asked looking in the rearview mirror.

Grandma nodded, revealing glistening gold teeth.

"Good, Da," the boy answered.

"This is a fine car you own," she said to his father.

"Thank you, mother," he responded, calling her "mother" though she wasn't, but thought the boy, because she was so old.

"Mama," the boy's mother said from the passenger seat, "do you feel dizzy?"

"I feel fine, and pleased in such comfort," her mother smiled.

"I'm sorry Mama that the trip is taking longer than we thought."

"I'm enjoying the ride very much," she answered.

"How many hours has it been?" the boy's mother asked his father.

"We left at noon, and it's eight."

"And we're still far, no?"

"Yes. Bad luck all this road work and traffic backup."

"We'll need to stay somewhere. Look for signs of a place to stay," she turned to her son. "A hotel or something."

"A hotel?" the boy sat up. It would be the first time. He pictured a plush, modern one like the hotels in the movies on TV. Uniformed men took their suitcases, uniformed elevator operators asked their floor, endless white carpets covered the rooms. Music played all the time, and there'd be something called "room service" to try. "Will it have a swimming pool?"

"And a skating rink," his father teased.

"Look for signs," his mother said.

"Do you want to lean against me while you look?" his grandmother smiled.

He knelt on the seat, leaned on her, and her padding gave like the feathered pillows and mattress he slept on at her house. As soon as he looked out the rolled down window, he announced something odd. "There's a little boy dancing on a roof."

"That could be dangerous," Grandma said.

"Where?" his mother asked.

"On an old house we just passed."

"It just looked like that to you," his mother said.

"I'm sure you saw right," his grandmother smiled to him.

"And a sign," the boy said. "I just saw a sign pass that said rooms. Rooms and a money number ten."

"Ten? Couldn't be," said his mother.

"Bargain," his father said.

"There on the ground, look," he said, "another paper sign, made like by a kid. It said the same, with an arrow pointing right."

"Why not see?" Grandma suggested.

"There's the turn," the boy's mother said.

His father turned the wheel and they traveled up a street without buildings on either side for blocks, or trees or grass, then stopped.

"There's nothing here," his mother said.

"There's that house over there." The boy pointed to a large old house with wraparound porch and many gables. Alone. Not even telephone polls near. "It's the house the little boy was dancing on."

"What a lovely old house," Grandma said.

"I don't know. It looks in need of care," said her daughter.

"Sometimes they're what's warmest inside," Grandma responded.

"Look. Another one of those paper signs," the boy pointed. "Like a kid drew. Knocked down."

"Let's look," his father said turning the wheel, and they approached a house thought the boy that looked like ones on Halloween drawings.

Parked in front, all except Grandma stepped out of the car.

"Look Grandma!" the boy turned to her, "at the upstairs window – the little boy!"

Her eyes lifted and roamed the many second and third floor windows. "I'm sorry child, but he must have left and I missed him. We'll see him inside."

A tall man, lanky like a skeleton in a checkered shirt and worn blue jeans stood waiting for them at the open screen door of the front porch.

"Ask him if this is the house renting rooms," the boy's mother instructed her son in their native language while walking up the sagging wood porch steps.

"Howdy, folks," he waved. Saw the signs? Rooms ten bucks? We make breakfast too. Home cooked vittles fresh-made every mornin' by my daughter."

"Hello," the boy's father nodded.

"How is – are you," the boy's mother smiled.

"Foreigners, ahy? You're welcome here. Come on in."

"You has two?" the boy's mother asked then turned to her son, "two –"

"Two rooms?" said the old man. Two, three, many as you want. Place's empty 'ceptin me an' my daughter."

"And the little boy," added the boy.

"No. Just us two. But you're son," he turned to his parents, "can fit in a room with you. No need buyin' a second room."

"For my grandmother," the boy said.

"Oh. Where's she?"

"In the car."

The man stretched his neck and saw the lady's profile framed in the back seat window. "Why… Why didn't you say so. Let me help the lady," and moving crab like, he hunched down the porch steps and to the car, opened the door, extended his hand to Grandma, then escorted her to the front door. "Now you be careful, madam, there's lots 'a steps and turns in this big old house. But you'll find she's still a loving place. Give 'er that. Cares for age and her guests, and will watch over you."

Grandma smiled and gestured a slow nod.

"How 'bout luggage?"

"Luggage?" the boy's father paused and turned to his son. "Luggage?"

The boy's shoulder's shrugged.

"Suitcases," said the old man.

The boy translated.

"Oh," his father said. "I –" and he moved toward the steps.

"That's my job," said the old man joining him.

"Has one only."

"Oh, okay big guy. Then I'll see to your family. Oh, and mister, thanks for droppin' in. We can sure use the money. Thank you."

"Thank you," the boy's father grinned.

*

For the boy's and his family's baths, the old man heated water in a giant pot in the yard over a wood fire the way cowboys and boy scouts did. The wood came from car-high piles in the yard the old man said came from knocked down neighboring houses and trees. The boy's father swore his bath, in a whale-sized tub on bent legs, was the best darn bath since leaving his country.

"What a soothing soak," the boy's mother purred of her own.

"Captured wood smoke in hot water," his father claimed.

"I don't know how that bony man carried so many pails of water upstairs," said Grandma. "A hard worker. I hope you'll tip him," she said to her son-in-law.

"I already tried. Wouldn't take it. Said tomorrow if we're satisfied with our stay, he'd appreciate it. Shared a cigarette with him. Pulled on it with such gusto, it's a balm to watch. I think his circumstances don't afford him many smokes."

"In my prayers tonight I'm keeping him," said Grandma feeling her gold medallion between her fingers. "Mercy on his obvious suffering, reprieve from his hardship. So little of Thy Grace, O Lord, Thine wretched creatures long. To heal, to become whole again."

When night fell, the old man lit lamps he called "kerosene lamps" in the dark halls and the two guest rooms. "Town knocked down the 'lectric polls. Phone lines too. So we manage with kerosene. Kinda' homey, I say."

His daughter, Hanna, hadn't appeared. The old man claimed she retired to her room just as they arrived. "Daughter's a little delicate. Always been. Rests a lot. But she'll be up bright 'an early to fix you the best breakfast you can imagine. That is if your 'magination don't wander far from sawbuck bacon 'n eggs, oatmeal, and pan fried bread. How you like your eggs tomorrow, youngster?" he turned to the boy.

"Any way."

"Like 'em scrambled?"

Scrambled, the boy heard and nodded. He never ate eggs scrambled and couldn't picture them. His mother made them some other way, though he didn't know its name. "Scrambled," tough men in the movies asked for theirs.

The old man led them up the cricking steps to Grandma's room. "Not much furniture. Sold most, 'long with paintings and such. But no bugs! That's guaranteed." He lit her lamp from his and placed it on the nightstand. "'Night, madam. And just sos you know, case you need anything, I'll be in the kitchen downstairs all night. I don't much sleep," and he turned to the boy, "you tell that to your grandma," and the boy did, and his grandmother nodded a smile to the man, as the boy's mother kissed her goodnight.

The man then led his three remaining guests to the adjacent room, lit their lamp, and bid them sound sleep. And changing into his pajamas, the boy listened to the old man's footsteps crick down the ragged edged stair runner to the first floor.

His mother drew the drapes open "so there's light from the full moon should you wake in the middle of the night." She tucked his blanket in, kissed his forehead, and the boy's back sank into a dough like mattress that swallowed his body.

His tired eyes tended the mellow light on the opposite wall. His drowsing mind missed how much time later came the rap on the bedroom door.

He waited for his parents to answer. They did not stir.

The rapping continued.

"Mommy," he whispered.

She did not reply.

Just as he thought the rapping stopped, it started again.

"Mommy."

She did not reply.

He slid from between the sheets and tiptoed to the door. "Who is it?"

No answer.

"Is it the little boy?"

One rap.

"Are you lost?"

Rap.

"Are you afraid?"

Rap-rap-rap the knocks increasingly echoed.

"Do you need help?"

Rap, the reply echoed like a drumbeat.

The boy turned the door lock's knob, and the bolt snapped open. Peering through the door crack, he sighted nothing, then opened the door wider. The doorway stood empty. "Little boy?" he murmured.

Raps sounded down the dark hallway. A lamp lit from that direction, and the boy observed a shadow move in the cast glow.

His head tilted out the doorframe, and at the end of the hall saw the little boy, a tiny boy really, standing square, facing him, kerosene lamp on the floor.

"You're the little boy on the roof and in the window. I saw you before."

The little boy raised his arm and lowered it.

"Is that nice man your grandpa?"

The little one nodded, and when he did, just as when he raised his arm, the boy thought he heard tiny gears, like from his battery-powered erector set.

Again the little boy raised and lowered his hand.

"Mommy," the boy whispered back to the room. No response, he closed the door and edged along the wall toward the boy. As he walked, he noticed lighter color rectangles on the wall, as if paintings or pictures once hung there.

"Do you want to shake hands?" the boy asked.

The little boy's head nodded and the boy confirmed the meshing gears came from him. And at arms length, more gears hummed as the little boy's jaw spread and his mouth opened wide, wide, wide until gleaming white spikes grew from the little boy's pink gums. When his eyes opened, red-hot beams shot at the boy's face, and squinting, the boy saw the little boy approach him on rollers. He saw spiked jaws open and close. The little rolling boy hissed when he exhaled, gurgled from the back of this throat when he inhaled. "I am Robot Henry, boy, and I am going to take you."

Blood streamed from Robot Henry's hollow teeth. Pointed ears stood up like on a snarling black Doberman.

Inching back, the boy's feet caught the ends of his pajamas and slipped on the buffed wood floor.

Robot Henry's arm lifted the kerosene lamp's handle. His mechanical head rotated, exhaled on the lamp flame and blew out the light at the same time his burning eyes shut. The boy thought a blanket was tossed over his head, one his pumping feet slipped on attempting to flee.

Mommy," he called. "Mommy," he implored turning the first doorknob his hands found. The door opened, he ran in and flew onto the bed. "Mommy! Mommy!"

"Child! Child! What's wrong? It's a dream. You're dreaming. It's a dream, my boy. There, there. It's a dream."

"Robot Henry, Grandma. Robot Henry," the boy cried.

"I know. I know."

"The little boy. Outside. He came. To take me. He's not good, Grandma. He's not good. Bad, he's bad."

"I know. I know. There, there. It's all right now. He's gone. He's gone now."

His arms held her like a shipwrecked sailor a tree stump, one of soft pulp, and lavender scented lace. Her Virgin Mother's medallion pressed against his face.

"He's gone now child. All is back to how it was. He's gone."

"He's not outside? Waiting?"

"He's all gone, now. All gone. Listen... Do you hear him?"

"...No..."

"Listen again. Anything?"

"...No. He's gone."

"Want to stay with me?"

"Yes, Grandma."

The drapes were closed, and the lamp out in her room, but the touch was hers, and the giving embrace. And when she kissed his cheek, her smile spread as hers did, small, long remaining.

Then… later… the boy, roused from a dream walking through flowers with smiles like his mother's, and a billowing sky of smokestack ships floating through cloud waterfalls. His fingers rubbed for his grandmother's medallion but found his palm empty. His hand spread and grasped the sheets searching for the charm, the necklace, his guardian's black laced padding.

He heard tiny gears mesh. Nearby. First, one set, then several – across the bedside. Two red coals smoldered. "Looking for someone?"

"Get away. My Grandma is coming."

"Tisk, tisk, tisk. Don't you know? Your grandmother I took away already. And now I'm coming – for you!"

The boy kicked at Robot Henry.

"Yes you! Ha, ha, ha, ha, ha."

""Away!" the boy shouted and kicked, fell on the floor and scampered toward the door. Below Henry's burning eyes, he saw the robot's claws shut on his pajama ends and seize them as his chomping jaws neared his pedaling feet.

"Let go! Let go!"

"Ha, ha, ha, ha! HA, HA, HA, HA, HA!"

Walking on his palms, the boy scuttled toward the door, but Henry's claws manacled to his pajama legs, he dragged the cleaving jaws as well.

"Ha, ha, ha, ha. Grandma is good, but a chicken so much better, ha, ha, ha, ha."

"Grandma! Grandma!"

"Ha, ha, ha, ha."

As the boy's swinging arm brushed the doorknob, his fingers wrapped around a pole, drew it close, then forced the broom against Robot Henry's chest. Pushing and stabbing Henry's neck and chest, his pajama legs slid from Henry's vice grip.

The boy turned the doorknob, ran out and slammed the door shut, and seeing light in the kitchen below, dashed down the stairs.

"Grandma! Grandma!" he called running into her arms. "Robot Henry! Robot Henry!"

"Holy Christ," declared the old man sitting in a chair opposite Grandma, and spilling his milk mug.

"My boy. My boy. The little robot again? There, there. Oh, I shouldn't have left you."

"He's in our room. Robot Henry. He said he took you. He's after us. Run. We have to run."

"Well I wish I knew your language," the old man said, "but I think I better go take a look."

"Gill," the boy's grandmother said, and the old man paused. Her head signaled toward a pan on the stove, and he stopped and sat back in his chair, his elbows leaning on its back. "Buck, how 'bout some warm milk with honey? Fixes anything, in my vast experience. Huh?"

The boy nodded, and the lanky old man heated milk already in a saucepan over a wood burning stove. "Your grandmother and me don't sleep much, sos we've been here talkin' a spell. Kinda' funny we not speakin' the same language, but holy darn if we don't understand just about everything we each say."

"His name is Gill," his grandmother said to her grandson in his first language. "He was born in this house. Married, added the porch, extra rooms, had and raised his children here."

"Your grandmother came down after it seems you had that dream with Robot Henry."

"It wasn't a dream."

"Think not?"

"He's up there now. Waiting for us."

"You think so?"

"Yes."

"You sound pretty sure. Sip that warm milk, take the mug, and let's have a look."

The old man reached out his hand to the boy in his grandmother's embrace, sitting in a slat-backed chair.

"Come on. I'll take my huntin' knife," he said, sliding out a knife like Davy Crocket used on TV against the bear.

The three held hands and walked to the stairs.

"Well I'll be," the old man said. At the top of the steps, right on the edge stood Robot Henry still as a statue.

"You see. It wasn't a dream."

The old man started up the squeaking stairs, ambling as if he would fall before each stride.

"Don't get too close," warned the boy.

"Not much chance him wantin' a bony specimen like me."

The boy wrapped his arms around his grandmother.

"Robot Henry," said the old man, "what the hell you want scarrin' a good little boy like that?" And when the old man reached to take Henry, the boy squeezed his grandmother's side and pushed his eyes against her dark robe.

The man brought Henry down, sat on a step and rested the little gadget on his knee. "Robot Henry, now what are we going to do with a misbehaving little boy like you? Huh?"

"You see. He wasn't a dream."

155

"Well, I don't know, Buck. Don't you remember before goin' to bed last night, he was on the mantel and I showed him to you? I told you I built him with two of my girls, the Good Lord keep them, an' you said he was mighty scary. You spotted him on the roof an' window, and I said he'd been known to do that, he was a bad little fella – once found 'em on the roof myself? Recall?"

"Yes…"

"Well, that just turned into a nightmare is all."

"But he'll come again. I know it."

"Think so, huh?"

He nodded.

"Well then we'll just have to do somethin' about that. Come on to the living room."

In the living room, the old man stationed the kerosene lamp on the mantel, then poked the embers in the fireplace with an iron, and tossed in kindling. "Give that a sec to catch good. Buck, you know what they used to do to the bad folks 'round here in the old days, and in the old country I guess?"

"Hang them?"

"Yeah," the old man chuckled, "the bad ones. But the really bad ones. The ones with a bad soul, they burned 'em. Burned 'em at the stake. You ever learn that?"

156

"Like to witches?"

"Exactly. Well, I figure, Robot Henry here is like one of them evil witches what cast a spell on you, an' so we got to burn 'em. Hangin's too good for 'em, I say. Sooo…" Unscrewing the cap from his kerosene lamp, the old man sprinkled liquid on a rag he drew from his back pocket and placed over Robot Henry. "And now, we'll lay ol' Henry here to rest and burn the badness out 'a him." He moved to lay Henry on the fire.

"Will he die?"

"A fiery death fer-sure. You don't mind, do ya?"

"I, I."

The boy looked up at his grandmother. Her hand brushed the back of his head, and he thought the glow from the fire on her gold teeth made them look like a saint's smile.

"Well?" asked the old man. "We can't wait any longer. Do we burn 'em?"

"Maybe he'll turn good without killing him."

"How, you figure?"

"Maybe if we're kind to him, maybe he'll become good. Maybe if we show him kindness, then he'll know how to be. He won't need to take anybody away, because he'll already have somebody."

The old man slid the rag off Henry's face and tossed it on the embers. They consumed it like hungry hands stripping bare a shank, and the three watched it vanish.

"I think you're way is best, Buck. Take Henry. You can hold him now 'cause I think you taught him it's easy to be bad, like we was gonna be when we were afraid. But that you're not afraid takin' a chance on him to become good. I think because Henry now knows we care about him, he's gonna turn good. Here, you take 'em."

The boy accepted Robot Henry. "But what if he comes again?" he asked his grandmother.

"You give him your hand, and you say I will love you."

"Will that do?"

"…Yes."

The boy handed Henry to the man. "You can put him back."

The man took Henry and stood him on the mantle, where he stayed, immobile, the night.

*

Fried bacon wafting through Grandma's bedroom door overtook the boy's gladdened dreams of Good Robot Henry. He remembered scrambled eggs, and his eyes snapped open. Drapes drawn to a bright day, Grandma's bag sat packed on a chair, her hairbrush atop a black wool shawl spread along its back.

He ran to his parent's room, splashed water on his face from a basin on the dresser, and bolted to the kitchen, where his family sat at a table, each in a different type of mended chair.

"Buck, I want you to meet my daughter, Hanna," the old man said.

"Hanna, this here's Buck – not his real name, but that's what I call 'em, and he don't mind."

"Hi," the boy said to a woman old as his mother.

Holding a frying pan by the stove, she nodded and her mouth moved but uttered only low "uh, oh, uh oh," it sounded like to the boy.

"She don't speak, Buck. She says she's glad to meet you. She was born with no tongue. But you can see what she has for ya'. You're scrambled eggs!"

Hanna turned, and the boy saw a puffy yellow mound; his finally revealed eggs the way tough men ate them.

"…Thank you."

"And one other thing, Buck, Hanna's got somethin' to tell you. Hanna…"

She set down the pan and took the boy's hand. Her chin dug into her chest. Her eyes lowered and rose. Her mouth uttered many "uh" and "oh."

The boy's hunger slipped.

Hanna's father remarked, "She says she's sorry for teasin' you with Robot Henry. She was just tryin' to have a little fun with ya's all. It explains how I kept finding the darn thing on the roof and all over. Hanna set Henry on the steps last night, and says she's sorry to scare ya'. And she and I, we're thankful to you for sparin' his life, 'cause she says he's her friend, and good after all."

While the old man and his daughter's guests ate, he only smoked – from the pack the boy's father gave him – and told them that ever since his wife died, they'd watched all the houses around them sold and bulldozed so a company could build new ones. That's why they had no electricity, telephones or hot water.

He refused to sell and move. His wife's grave was out back, and she still lived there. Not really lived there but he felt like she did, and once the house was torn down, she'd be gone for good, and really die, and what matter then that he could afford electricity and things if he'd lose all he really cared about. It "wasn't worth the trade," he said. "Wasn't a fair bargain," he claimed.

His daughter felt the same, he said. She spoke with her mother all the time in the big old house, and couldn't think of losing where her mother lived, and where they'd always been together, talked, every corner filled with memories. "Be like bein' a ghost, but in reverse. Like you have a body, but the world's gone. Like one big toothless, useless set 'a gums."

As they all stepped onto the front porch, shading their brows from the new sky's rays, the boy heard his father cry, "Ohhh," and all looked and saw their car, shiny, gleam.

"You'll look real dandy drivin' up to the falls in a freshly washed automobile."

"Look beautiful. Thank you, sir."

"'Ceptin you like the falls so much, you don't wanna leave, I hope you'll consider all stayin' with us on your way back. We sure would like that. Cut you a discount. We're like distant family now."

*

"Grandma?" the boy asked his grandmother later in their rambling car. He rested against her smooth black blouse, one now not all black, but with hundreds of tiny white polka dots she called moons. "Grandma?"

She blinked then smiled.

"Will we stop at the old man's house on our way back?"

"I hope so," she said. "But I have a feeling we won't see them again."

"They'll be gone?"

"They'll be gone."

"His wife too?"

"Wherever he is, she'll be."

"Not in the house when it's knocked down?"

"She'll go wherever he goes."

"So, he can leave?"

"He's told himself he can't. But he'll have to, and he'll find then, she's always with him."

"You mean like in heaven?"

"There, but before then, with him, beside the girl too. Like Grand-Da with me."

"Grand-Da's with you?"

"He is. Here, and everywhere. And when my house falls, and my furniture goes, and my shiny gold teeth return to the ground," she smiled, "he and I will rejoin, in the best way, like rivers to the ocean, like mist once sky and sea."

"Look, Grandma! There, there in those clouds! Do you see the falls?"

"Where?"

"Those clouds. There. I see the great falls. Do you?"

"…Yes."

The Bicycle Ride

The boy had long ago outgrown his first bicycle. He no longer admired how his knees brushed the handlebar, or that he carried it with one hand up the stairs to his parent's row house apartment. Squatting in it, he thought he looked like a first grader playing leapfrog. Maneuvering it now in between sidewalk games of box ball, girls skipping rope, uncollected garbage cans, and the worst – mothers strolling beside their ice cream licking children – he thought was like walking a pirate plank blindfolded. But guiding his bike while he held a milk container in each hand, was as if the jittery plank contained traffic, in both directions, on the high seas, in a storm.

On the sidewalk ahead, a boy's pink rubber ball tossed against stoop steps, struck a bluestone step edge, and the stoopball player skittering back, back, back to catch the beaner, met the boy's wobbling front wheel.

The two boys moaned holding their sides and limbs while ambling to their feet.

"Look what you did!" the boy said.

"Look what *you* did!" said the stoopball player pointing a chafed elbow at his assailant.

"That's nothing, you little baby. A little scrape. Look at what *you* did." And he lifted a milk container in each hand, milk dripping out their bottom edges.

So? You could have killed somebody."

"I should kill *you*, if you don't pay for these. Mrs. Klay won't take them like this."

"I'm not paying. You should watch where you're going."

"I *was* watching where I was going. You ran into me!"

"You crashed into *me*!"

"You stupid –" and just before uttering a word to damn him at Holy Confession later that Saturday afternoon, "idiot" rescued him.

"You're the stupid idiot."

"You are."

"You are."

The boy noticing his scuffed knee starting to bubble blood, raised it to blow on. "You are."

"I got a tissue. If you want," the other boy said.

The boy's hand extended, and the other boy placed a lint covered pink tissue in it. "It's my mother's. Makes me keep one in my pocket."

"Thanks," the boy said patting his knee.

"How come you don't ride a bigger bike?"

"I'm getting one when I finish grade school and we move to the suburbs this summer," the boy said blowing on the scrape.

"Hurt?"

"No. Yours?"

"Nah. How you expect to steer holdin' two quarts of milk?"

"My hands grew since I started running errands for Mrs. Klay in the second grade."

"Not enough looks like."

"So, are you going to pay?"

"I don't have enough money."

"You have any?"

The other boy drew his hand from his pocket, examined his palm, and turned it over onto the boy's outstretched hand. "That's all I got."

"It's, ah, enough for one, and I have the change Mrs. Klay usually lets me keep, and some other change. That should buy two."

The other boy turned the bicycle's handlebar, lifted the bicycle to its wheels, and held it steady.

Holding the milk containers by their lids, the boy straddled the held bicycle, glanced at the handrail, the long milk quarts, and said, "Here, you take them," and reached the containers to the other boy.

"What am I supposed to do with them?" the other boy said accepting the leaking containers.

"You drink milk don't you?"

"Yeah, but these are dripping."

"Give them to your mom. She'll put them in a pot or something. I have to go back to Millers for a couple of new ones."

"I'll put 'em in a pot or something 'till she gets home."

"That was a good beaner."

"Caught it too.

"You count them twenty-five points?"

"Yeah."

"Sorry I hit you."

"I'll look out for you on your way back."

"Bye."

"See 'ya."

The boy peddled quickly back to Millers Grocery, dashed to the rear, removed two quarts of milk from refrigeration, paid with his last coin, and re-met his dilemma: grasping the carton folds using the same hands that controlled the bicycle.

Why did he always have to leave playing street ball when Mrs. Klay called him to run an errand just because his mother said he must, he griped? This time it was the street-title stickball game he was missing, and the reason he had attempted the errand in one trip.

He tried holding one quart under an arm. It did not work. With rope he spotted at the curb, he tied the cartons to the seat. They almost fell. He squeezed a quart under each arm. Each instance, he traveled part of a block before he lost control of the bicycle and almost crashed or dropped the cartons.

Finally, unbuckling his belt, he pulled his pants waist, forced the quarts in, and cautiously striding, found the solution. Until, rushing out from an alley to the sidewalk, there appeared the street's adolescent boy gang. Blocking his way, the U Cs teasingly jostled him, and the bicycle and he fell to the concrete.

"Oh, the poor boy fell off his bike," said Huck, the U Cs' leader.

"Flat on his face," laughed Duck.

"Bound to happen, ridin' a little girl's bike," scoffed Ruck.

First, the boy thought the fall burst his stomach. It felt all wet there. Then he remembered the milk and saw a carton flattened against his midsection.

What happened next the boy did not expect. He had never fought anyone, never hit another boy, nor thought he could. Instead of thanking the U Cs leader when Huck lifted the bicycle, his legs coiled and arms pincered against the ground like a cat preparing a leap. He surged onto Huck, his fingernails scraping his face, his hands unexpectedly forming fists. His arms swung at and struck Huck, until lowered to his knees, his forearms protecting his head, Huck yelled "Stop. Stop. Stop it kid. Stop."

The watching U Cs' fists opened, and their arms slid to their sides.

"I'm sorry," Huck cried.

The boy stopped swinging.

"Cut it out," said Duck.

"Yeah," Ruck said. "He said he was sorry."

The beating ended, Huck's elbows lowered from his head, and he stood taking a step back from the clenched fist boy. "Sorry. I'm sorry. We were only kidding. Just havin' some fun."

Duck and Ruck noticed the darker color material running down the boy's trousers. "Is that...?" said Duck.

"You...ah? Ruck questioned.

The boy's hands passed over his pants. "It's milk."

"Milk?"

"The milk I was carrying."

"Oh. Oh!" said Ruck relieved.

"Cool. That's cool," nodded Duck.

The boy surveyed the ground around his feet. "You stupid... stupid... idiots," he said head hanging.

"We're sorry man," said Huck. "Sorry."

"Yeah, sorry man. Sorry," the others said.

"We'll get you new ones," said Huck picking up a leaking milk container.

"I don't have any more money," the boy said.

"That don't matter," said Huck. "How'd you like to be a U C?

"A, U C?"

"Yeah. One of us. What do you think, guys," Huck turned to the others.

"Yeah. He can join. We can use a fourth member."

"What do I have to do?" the boy asked.

"Nothin'. You was just voted in. Congratulations."

"But you need a name. A club name."

"Has to be like, Huck, Ruck."

"Or Duck."

These were the kids the boy avoided from the street. All the boys avoided them. Fearless and feared he was told they were, and he told himself. When riding his bike or walking home from school, he worried about meeting them. When he spied them across a street, he looked away, walked faster, and hoped they had not seen him. Once when Huck struck his leg with a fired snowball containing a rock, he told himself it didn't hurt, that Huck did not mean it, and he limped home.

He also knew in a way he did not understand, that what they did, running wherever they wanted, cursing when they liked, even smoking cigarettes as he once saw them, adventurous things to do. "Buck," he answered.

"Buck. That's cool," Huck smiled."

"I almost picked that," said Ruck. "That's cool."

"Yeah, cool. Real cool," said Duck.

"Welcome to the club, Buck," said Huck putting out his hand. "No hard feelings, right?"

"No," the boy said.

"Hey, you better get home an' change." said Duck.

"Yeah," Ruck said. "You don't want somebody to think," he laughed. "I mean, you're a U C now. Got to keep up appearances."

"What about my milk for Mrs. Klay?"

"That old nagging hag?"

The boy had never heard anyone speak like that of Mrs. Klay, he reflected. He knew her all his life. She and Dad Klay cared about him and about his mother and father. "I have to finish my errand," came his voice low.

"That's all right, man," said Huck. "Duck, Ruck. Run to Millers and get Buck two quarts of milk and catch up with us. Hurry up."

The two ran toward Millers Grocery.

Huck gave the boy the bike. He took the handlebars and together they walked saying nothing more.

As they approached Mrs. Klay's next door to the boy's row house, the boy looked up at the windowsill she always rested her pale fleshy arms on, and did not see her.

Ruck and Duck soon reached them with two fresh quarts of milk.

"I can't pay you now," the boy said.

"It's cool, man," said Ruck. "It's on the house."

"Millers," Duck laughed.

"We'll see you tomorrow, Buck," Huck said, "we got to go."

"Bye."

"See ya' man. See ya' Buck," they said pushing and teasing one another as they knocked about moving up the street, their laughter lingering in the boy's ears.

He brought the milk upstairs to Mrs. Klay and Dad. Unlike what he usually did, stay and have a glass of milk and plate of cookies Mrs. Klay made daily, he said his mother needed him, and left.

His mother did not really need him, and he did not try to find out, instead, turning before entering their second floor apartment, he climbed the wall ladder to the roof.

He pushed the metal roof cover, stepped onto the flat blacktop surface, and contemplated the garage roofs and buildings around their house. Wishing to see farther, he started up the narrow, vertical iron ladder on Mrs. Klay's roof that Dad Klay's ham radio antenna traveled.

Higher than the street trees, atop the ladder he never thought he'd climb, he scanned black tar and silver painted roofs, water tanks and antenna thatches, and farthest away, orange yellow sky that meant his father would soon be home.

From his shirt pocket he drew a cigarette Huck gave him on their walk home. His fingers slid over the paper, then passed it under his nose and he inhaled. He thought of dropping it and watching it tumble to the sidewalk. From out a window, he heard his mother call his name. He passed the unlit cigarette again under his nose. His mother called his name again for dinner. His father was home. Again, he heard his name.

He looked at the antenna sea, sun setting beyond, breathed he thought the freshest air anywhere, up there so high. A breeze roused the tree leaves. His fingers slid the soft white stub behind his ear. His hands grabbed the ladder rails.

16540738R00103

Made in the USA
Middletown, DE
16 December 2014